AM_____ ___

WAND

Book Two of
SPIRALS OF TIME

Margaret Iggulden

THREE OAK LEAVES PRESS

First edition published in 2023 by Three Oak Leaves Press.

Print ISBN 978-1-7397839-2-1
Ebook ISBN 978-1-7397839-3-8

Cover artwork by Angela Davis

Cover design by Clarkes Printing, Monmouth

For my aunt, Eileen

The Amethyst Wand

CONTENTS

Chapter 1
At Hartland House

June 25th

Last night I had that dream again...

In front of me, a crystal hovered; shimmering, sparkling. Purple, it was; long, pointed, threads of red running through it.

I stretched out my hand to grasp it; it moved away, fading into shadows.

A voice. The Goddess.

'Tara – Guardian of the Bronze Mirror – your second task awaits you. This will be more perilous than the first. You will be greatly tested. Not only you, but your twin, David, and your cousin, Simone. Tread this path with care...

All must be brave. All must be strong. Remember your mission – to save Planet Earth from destruction. The oceans must be cleansed. The air must be made pure again. All must be in harmony. For every life, every breath, is precious; each tree, each bird, animal and insect, all of Nature.

Unless you find the second crystal – unless you cast it into the waters – this world will die.

This time has been chosen for you to complete the task.

Beware of enemies. Beware of those who serve the Warrior God, Mars.'

Images came and went. Roman soldiers marching, fighting with swords, with spears... All appeared, then vanished.

The Goddess spoke again: 'See the might of the Roman Empire...'

Fiery eyes appeared; glaring, glowering. A figure holding a spear and a shield... two horses and a chariot...

Later:

We're at Hartland House, at Nanny Lita's and Grandpa Osian's for a few days. Just below is Caerleon and a Roman fort. Is that where Mars, the Warrior God, waits for us? I'm feeling nervous – but we were chosen for this quest. And I'm the peacemaker. It's such a pressure. Everyone sees me as calm and cool.

But it's tough.

Simone gets so moody. Will she keep our pact, to help save the Planet? And my twin. Will David spill secrets – and get into trouble again? It needs all of us to search for the crystal; all of us to save our beautiful planet. But will we succeed this time?

Tara thrashed around in bed, muttering, 'So cold... icy... Planet Kircus...'

Wrapping the duvet tightly around herself, she rolled over, crying out, 'Quest... save the planet... Second task. More dangerous. Goddess... She's holding something, showing me something; purple, glowing.' She shouted, 'Oh those eyes! Burning! Red, orange, staring at me. Mars! God of War! He's here!'

Tossing from side to side, she called out, 'Where is this? Small, gloomy, eerie. Bones, so many bones. A child – reaching out, she's begging for help...'

Tara curled up into a ball. 'But what can I do? No. That's too difficult... Now I see... a circle of oaks. A woman whispering – chants? Spells? A man by a fire – hot, blazing, hammering long shapes... Crashing from the woods... Danger!'

She sat up, her eyes wide open. 'Run! Down this track... Argh! I'm falling... The Bronze Mirror – spinning... out of my hand... I mustn't lose it – I can't lose it...'

Twisting and turning, she struggled to catch it.

'Tara!' Someone was shaking her shoulder. 'Wake up!'

'The Mirror... so precious...'

'Tara! Wake up! You're having a bad dream.'

She rubbed her eyes. It was still dark in the tiny bedroom.

'Simone? What...? Where are we?'

'At Hartland House. With Nanny Lita and Grandpa Osian.'

Her cousin picked up the duvet from the floor and put it back over her.

'*Alora!* Every night you have this terrible dream.'

Tara sighed; she felt under the pillow for her bag. The Bronze Mirror was inside. *It's here. It's safe. Why do I keep having the same nightmare?*

Smells of toast and scrambled eggs wafted up the stairs. Tara turned over; her eyes focused on a wall of purple flowers. Early sunlight streamed through the bedroom window; yellow checked curtains, a dark brown wardrobe.

'Tara! David! Simone!' called Nanny Lita. Breakfast is ready! Come on! You're going to Caerleon today! Exciting!'

'Off to see the amphitheatre,' said Osian.

A groan came from the next bed.

'Simone! Your grandpa's warming some croissants for you.'

'You'll need a few of these for your long walk

down the hill!'

'A perfect start to her day!' said Nanny Lita.

Tara grinned as her cousin muttered, '*O Dio mio...*'

Snuggling down again, she listened to their grandparents chuckling together in the kitchen.

'And there's blackcurrant jam – your favourite,' their grandmother called up.

'Not porridge. *Bene!* Good!' said Simone.

'Thanks, Nanny Lita! We'll be down now,' said Tara, yawning.

Smoothing the lilac-flowered cover, she tried to remember the dream she'd had last night. She closed her eyes. *Was it the same one as the night before?*

'Did I talk in my sleep, cuz?'

'Talk! You were shouting! Again! Something about eyes, flaming eyes, spears, somewhere spooky... *Alora!* You woke me up!'

Tara reached for her journal. 'I'll write down what I can remember now.'

David strolled into their bedroom holding some leaflets. 'Morning! I found these – they're all about the Roman fortress. Maybe there'll be a re-enactment and we can dress up as Roman soldiers. That'd be cool!'

'What time is the bus to that city – Cardiff?' said Simone flinging on her dressing gown.

'We're going to Caerleon,' said Tara. 'And there isn't a bus from here.'

'Don't panic, cuz!' said David. 'It's all downhill!'

'Any shops there?' Simone stretched and put her feet on the floor. 'No!' She started dancing around. 'Argh! Ooooh!'

'What's the matter?'

Lifting up her foot, she stared at her toes; tiny brown pieces of something were stuck between them.

'Ugh! What are these?'

Tara laughed. 'Someone's been eating nuts!'

Bits of shell were scattered all over the floorboards.

'Has to be Bethan!' grinned Tara. 'Have you been teaching her to how to open walnuts, Twin?'

'No! Grandpa did last night! Isn't she the most amazing puppy?'

'*Cane catavi!* Bad dog!' Simone hissed, tiptoeing between the piles of shells.

'Where is she?'

David looked around. The spaniel was lying under a chair, staring up at them with her deep brown eyes.

Are they angry with me? Long dark hair girl is. Flashing eyes! I'll send her love. She gazed at Simone and wagged her tail.

'Come here, little dog,' said David, picking her up. 'Don't eat nuts in the bedrooms!'

Lowering his voice, he said, 'Sweep the shells under the beds next time with your nose, then no one will notice.'

Tara padded across to the window and drew the

curtains. Across the road, she could see the church tower.

'I love it here,' she said, looking at the chestnut trees swaying in the breeze.

'Me too. We'll come over in autumn and pick up lots of conkers!' said David.

'I've missed them so much,' sighed Simone.

'Conkers?'

She glared at David. '*No!* Seeing Nanny Lita and Grandpa Osian. Because I live in Rome – er – there are things I need to talk to them about. Many things.' She began twisting the end of her plait.

The young girl sighed deeply as she watched the twins sweep the pieces of shell into a pile and throw them into the waste bin.

'I've still got some bits between my toes.' Simone brushed more off. 'There.'

'Hey! Pick them up!' David called after her as she disappeared into the bathroom.

Tara shook her head. 'She must have been a queen in a previous lifetime.'

'I don't care who she was. She's a moaning Minnie!' David frowned. 'We made a pact at St Anne's Well last week, to help each other with this quest. We have to find the crystals and save the planet.'

'Maybe we can talk about how bees work together, help each other, for the good of the hive...'

'Be direct! And let's hope she won't give us too much grief!'

'Thanks! Why is it always me? I feel—'

'Breakfast!' called their grandpa.

David hurtled down the stairs, the spaniel scampering behind him.

'Great! I'm famished! Simone, I'm going to eat all your croissants!'

The kitchen was cosy; a whistling kettle was perched on top of an Aga, which looked as though it had been there for a hundred years. Next to the cooker stood a Welsh dresser with blue-and-white plates on the top shelf, cups and saucers below, and knick-knacks on the bottom. Photos covered all the walls: weddings, birthdays, holidays.

Elita and Osian fussed over their grandchildren.

'Have some more toast.'

'There'll be Welsh cakes and bara brith for tea. Your grandpa can look after the puppy for you today.'

Bethan's ears pricked up; she stared at David and whined.

'Sorry, Grandpa. She wants to come with us.'

'How about we take her for a walk around the village this evening?' said Tara.

'Or over towards the hillfort,' said Elita.

'Where's that?' David buttered a slice of toast. 'Is

it by the church tower?

'Last time we climbed all the way up and saw right across the estuary to Bristol,' said Tara.

'Totally awesome.'

David dropped some pieces of toast under the table for Bethan to nibble.

Simone wandered in, sat down, and peered at the pile of croissants.

'It was the hillfort of the Silures,' said Elita as she passed her granddaughter the jam.

'Who were they?'

'An Iron Age tribe – they lived around this area for hundreds of years.'

'Fierce they were,' added Osian. 'I always say—'

'– they've come back and now play rugby for Wales!' finished his wife.

The twins laughed while Simone looked puzzled.

'*Mi scusi.* How do we get to Caerleon?'

'There are the bikes,' said Elita.

'That's a good idea,' said Tara. 'We could whizz down—'

'*No!* Pushing them back up – it's too hard.' Simone frowned as she remembered struggling up the steep valley to Trellech a few days before. 'I mean, no thanks, Nanny Lita.'

'If you follow the path over to the hillfort, you can cut down through the woods and get to Caerleon that way,' said Osian.

'What's there?' asked Simone, taking another croissant.

Bethan moved further under the table. *Smells good. She might drop some...*

'The Roman Museum—'

'There's lots of things to see –' said Elita – 'statues of gods and goddesses, inscriptions on stone, helmets, swords...'

Simone rolled her eyes.

'Shields ...'

'Jewellery, too, and pottery.'

'Yes – those huge amphorae – and coins.'

The girl from Rome sighed.

'Cool,' said David. 'Do they let dogs in?'

'I'm not sure,' said his grandfather. 'You can go inside the barracks.'

'And there's a dig. Some archaeologists are excavating there this summer.'

'We love archeys!' said David.

'Just like home,' muttered Simone as she pushed her plate away.

A shadow fell over her face. 'Nanny Lita, have you spoken to Mamma since I came here?'

Her grandparents exchanged glances.

'Er – we don't know what their plans are – yet.'

'They've such a lot to sort out,' said her grandfather.

Elita flashed a warning look at her husband.

'What do you mean, Grandpa?'

'Your dad's busy. He can't leave Rome just yet.'

'Why not?' Simone made a face.

'Didn't he tell you?' asked Osian.

'You know those treasures they found last year, near the Pyramids – scarabs, jewellery?' said Elita.

'He's organising a new exhibition in the Egyptian museum,' said Osian.

'Awesome!' said David. 'I'd love to go to Egypt. Discover a lost tomb...'

He helped himself to more toast.

'And your mum will be touring New Zealand in November.' Elita smiled, adding, 'What a beautiful voice she has!'

Osian nodded. 'Juggling dates. It can get tricky.'

'It's not only that.' Simone wailed. 'No one ever listens to me. No one ever asks me what I want!'

David kicked his sister's ankle.

Twin! She sent him a mind-message. *Stop it!*

Tara stared hard at the large kitchen clock on the wall; the big hand jumped.

'I forgot!' Beaming at her grandchildren, Elita said, 'We found these old photo albums in the attic last week. Of you when you were babies. And your parents, too...'

She went over to the dresser, picked up several albums, and put them on the kitchen table.

'Great! I love seeing everyone in their old-fashioned clothes,' said Tara as she opened one. 'Don't you, Simone?'

Shrugging her shoulders, Tara's cousin went over to the window. Willow, the ginger-and-black cat, was curled up on the lawn; one eye fixed on two sparrows sipping water on the bird table.

Simone saw nothing; her eyes filled with tears.

'Leave her for now,' whispered her grandfather. 'Now, have a look at these.'

'Oh, totally retro!' David flicked through the pages. Some were torn at the edges. Underneath each snap was faded writing.

'Course you didn't have telly then!' he laughed.

'Yes, we did!'

Tara pointed to a picture of a young couple. 'Who are they, Nanny Lita? I can't make out the names.'

'My parents, Grace and Leonard. That was taken on St Lucia, just as they were leaving to emigrate here.'

'Our great grandma and pa! How cool is that?'

The twins gazed at the couple who were standing next to a huge ship.

'HMT *Empire Windrush*,' read Tara. 'When did they come here?'

'1948. After World War Two. The government invited them to work here, to help the country. So thousands left the Caribbean,' said Osian.

'Left those islands of Paradise: Jamaica, Barbados, St Lucia, to make a new life here,' added Elita.

'In cold, damp, rainy Britain!' said David.

'It took some getting used to! Your great-grandma was a nurse in Cardiff and great-grandpa drove buses in the city. Most went to London, others to Bristol.'

Elita took an album over to Simone. 'Look,

cariad. Here you are as a baby. So beautiful.'

She put her arm around her granddaughter whispering, 'Everything will be fine. You'll see.'

Nodding, Simone pointed to a silver framed photograph on the dresser.

'Is – is that you and grandpa on your wedding day, Nanny Lita?'

'It is! We met in Accident and Emergency! He'd tripped over a dog and broken his ankle.'

Osian smiled at his wife. 'And then she stole my heart!'

'You look very happy there,' said Simone.

'And so we were – we are,' smiled her grandmother.

'Being kind to each other. That's the secret,' said Osian.

'*Si.* Yes. That would make all the difference.'

'Hey, cuz!' said Tara holding up a photo. 'This has to be our mum and your mum, Auntie Fay. With fishing nets and glass jars!'

'Those cliffs look brilliant,' said David, peering over her shoulder.

'We visited a different beach on the Gower every day,' said Osian. 'Three Cliffs is my favourite.'

'Can we go there sometime?' said David. 'Bethan would love the sea.'

The puppy looked at him. *Are we going for a walk now?*

'Why not? We could go over to West Wales too, before the end of the holidays,' said Elita. 'What do you think?'

'Cool!'

'Amazing!'

'Hmm.' Simone reached for the orange juice.

Tara was examining the photo. 'Who do we look like? Our mums or our dads?'

Osian smiled. 'You're a perfect mix!' He tussled his grandson's dark, curly hair. 'This has to come from your Caribbean great-grandparents.'

'Osian's eyes are like yours, Tara – green,' said Elita. 'That's definitely Irish... a good dose of Country Waterford. Celtic blood!'

'And twins – your dad's family is from Orkney – so there has to be some Viking DNA in you both.'

'Brilliant!'

Elita smiled at them. 'You're both wonderful! Caribbean, Celtic, Viking, and a good dollop of Anglo-Saxon in there somewhere too, I expect!'

'A stupendous stew!' said David. 'We're truly awesome!'

'As indeed all human beings are,' added Osian.

'And me?' asked Simone, sniffing and reaching for a tissue. 'What about me?'

David looked up to the ceiling and sighed.

Elita stroked her granddaughter's hair. 'Ah, *cariad.* I was there when you were born. Held you when you were seconds old... Now – you look exactly like your mum when she was twelve.'

'I thought I was adopted,' Simone whispered.

'No, no.' Elita gave her a *cwtch.* 'Your eyes are

dark brown – Caribbean or Egyptian. Your straight, dark hair – that's from your father's side.'

'And his height,' said Osian. 'You're taller than the twins.'

'That's a good thing!' laughed Tara.

Simone took another croissant. 'You're right. It **is** a good thing. I wouldn't want to be short.'

David choked on some toast and spluttered.

'Our Egyptian princess, we called you, when you were a baby,' said Osian.

'No change there then,' muttered his grandson.

'Why don't we have our DNA done?' Tara said quickly, throwing her brother The Look.

'And our ancestry too,' said David. 'Early birthday presents?'

Simone began flicking through another album. 'Are there any of my parents together?'

'Yes, this was taken in the garden here.'

Under a cherry tree bursting with blossom, two young people were gazing into each other's eyes; a tall, handsome man, and a slim, vivacious woman.

'Mamma looks beautiful.' said Simone. 'And her dress is so *elegante*.'

'Effat looks very happy,' said her grandmother.

'He looks serious all the time now.' Simone sighed. 'Did my grandparents come over from Egypt when they got married? Have you got any photos of them?'

'I remember seeing some of your Egyptian family,' said Elita. 'I'll find them later today.'

'You can tell us who they all are,' said Osian.

Simone gulped. 'I–I haven't seen them for a long time.'

She's going to get upset again. Tara sent a mind-message to David. *Say something – quickly, Twin!*

David took a deep breath.

'I know! Let's visit your Egyptian family. Sail down the Nile! Search for a long-lost pharaoh's tomb...'

Simone bit her lip. '*Si. Bene.* Yes. Good.'

'See the Sphinx, the Pyramids, go inside the King's chamber...' Tara's eyes gazed off into the distance, 'stroll around Luxor, visit the Valley of the Queens – Queen Hapshepsut's temple—'

David broke in, 'I've always wanted to see that – truly cosmic! Then there's the Valley of the Kings... Tutankhamun...' He looked around the table. 'Could we go soon?'

The letter box clattered. Packages and a newspaper dropped onto the mat.

Bethan raced to the front door, barking.

'Look at the time!' said Elita. 'Here are your sandwiches. Cheese and tomato. Egg and cress. Apples. Fruit juices, water.'

'Take some energy bars, too – honey and nuts,' said Osian. 'Tara! Don't go without your bag.'

'Thanks, Grandpa,' said Tara, taking the bag from him. She felt the outline of the Bronze Mirror inside. *I've a feeling we're going to need this today.*

Chapter 2

The Portal Opens

Shutting the metal gate behind them, the twins, Simone and Bethan turned left down the hill to the stone steps that led into the churchyard. A wooden sign announced: 'Lodge Hill'.

The puppy was already pulling hard on her leash, snuffling around the graves on either side of the path.

Moss covered the old lettering. 'Doris Jenkins, 1921 – 1999. Dearly beloved wife of...' Yellow roses drooped in a black vase.

Ferns were beginning to unfurl on this warm summer day. Scampering across a branch, a grey squirrel paused to check out the green spiky conkers.

'I want to go into the church,' said Simone.

'Grandpa said there's a healing stone inside.'

'Then we won't have time to see everything in Caerleon,' said David. 'The amphitheatre, museum – and the barracks.'

Simone glared. 'I live in the middle of Rome! Arches, temples, columns – everywhere. *Molti* ruins!'

Taking a deep breath, Tara said, 'How about we visit the church tomorrow? We could climb the tower, see over to the estuary...'

'I want to go inside now.' Simone stalked up the gravel path.

Oh no! The day's only just begun, thought Tara, exchanging looks with her twin.

'I'll go on my own,' Simone called. 'You go to those old ruins. You don't have to look after me. And –' she shouted – 'stop talking about me like that.'

'Like what?' Tara was shocked.

'"O poor Simone. What a nuisance, she is." You both do it. Or think it. You talk about me in your heads. I know. I feel – er – *solo* – alone – left out. The next time there's a scary thing to do, you won't have to protect me. I won't be there!'

She tugged hard on the iron handle; the church door was locked. 'Argh!'

Slipping the leash, Bethan raced up the path and sat on the stone steps next to her. The spaniel nudged her leg with her nose. *I'll make her happy.*

Gulping back tears, Simone patted the top of the puppy's head.

David was furious. 'OK,' he called. 'I won't. It's just that you complain all the time. And go into moods—'

Tara grabbed his arm. 'Twin! Stop it! You're making this worse.'

'Well, she doesn't help with any chores,' he muttered. 'Or clear up after herself.'

'Chill. Her parents row a lot,' said Tara. 'It makes her miserable. She feels she's been dumped on us. Be kind. And if you can't think of anything kind to say, then – keep *schtum.*'

He gazed up at the clouds floating across the blue sky. 'OK. I'll try. I will. But admit it, Twin. She's hard work.'

Simone marched back down the path, kicking the gravel as she went. Bethan scampered by her side.

'The church – it is closed today.'

Tara put her arm around her cousin. 'We'll have a great time, you'll see. You can explain all the things in the museum to us. We don't know that much about the Romans.' She stared at her twin. 'Do we, David?'

'Er – I'm sorry, cuz.' He held out Bethan's leash. 'You can walk her if you want to. She – she likes you.'

Taking the leash, Simone went ahead. The spaniel trotted along beside her, sniffing at clumps of dandelions between the graves.

'I'm sorry, cuz,' he called after her. 'I am. Really!'

Simone opened the gate and disappeared out of

the churchyard. Her cousins stood watching her.

'Hey, Twin,' said Tara. 'Remember the quest. We can't let these silly rows get in the way. No anger, remember.'

David squeezed his fists together and pressed them against his eyes. 'Ergh! She's so annoying sometimes. But – I'll try.'

'And you can be a pain, too!'

They grinned at each other.

'Race you!'

Hurtling along the narrow track, they jumped over nettles and straggling briars. As they rounded a bend, they came to a holly bush. In front of them was a circle of ancient oaks; trunks gnarled and twisted, branches crooked, stretching up to the sky.

A place where the sun can't force its beams through. Tara shivered.

Simone was running around, calling, 'Bethan! Where are you? Come back!'

'Now what's happened?' muttered David.

Tara glanced around. There was no sign of the puppy.

'She pulled so hard on the leash. And – now she's run away. It's scary here. I—'

'She'll be back,' said Tara. 'She'll be down a hole, digging for a rabbit.'

'How difficult can it be to walk a dog?' muttered David.

'Try whistling for her, Twin.'

He took a deep breath; the next second, a series of long and short whistles came from his lips.

The girls stared at him in amazement.

'I've been teaching her Morse Code!'

He whistled again.

The spaniel came bounding out from the woods; she was covered in bits of twigs and dried-up leaves.

'Good girl!' David picked her up and stroked her head. 'We've been practising, haven't we?'

Making low, whining noises, the puppy struggled out of his arms and raced down a different track.

'Bethan! That's the opposite direction from Caerleon.'

Tara felt a cool wind on her face. High above them, dark grey clouds were sweeping across the sky.

She took the Bronze Mirror from her bag. There came a whisper:

Follow her to the place.
You must make haste.
The portal is opening,
The time – it is coming.

'The Mirror says we must follow her – quickly.'

'Good job she's micro chipped,' said David. 'Not that that'll make any difference – we're off to the past!'

'No! Oh no!'

'Come on, Simone!'

They ran along the path behind Bethan until she

stopped, sat, and refused to go any further.

Simone leant on a tree to catch her breath. *This bark – it's so rough to touch... And these old trees. Knots, whorls, like eyes, staring at me.* She shuddered. *This place is spooky...*

A single magpie flew up and into the trees.

One for sorrow, thought Tara.

'What can you smell, Bethan?' said David.

The puppy sniffed the air, snuffled left, then right. Down another track she shot; the trio raced to keep up with her.

Are we going around in a circle? wondered Tara.

Snagging themselves on brambles, brushing aside clumps of ferns, they chased after her through the woods and arrived at a clearing. In front of them was a grassy mound – high, long, overgrown with grasses and nettles. Bethan was sitting still, alert, listening. To what?

All was still. No birds sang.

Tara stared at the mound. *I've seen this before. Was it in my dream?*

'It feels scary here,' said Simone.

'Definitely eerie, cuz,' said David.

Rustling noises came from nearby bushes. Tara spun around. Nothing.

Is someone spying on us? I can feel eyes all around.

At the far edge of the mound, the spaniel began digging.

'What's she looking for?' asked Simone.

'Let's clear away these ferns and see,' said David. 'Do you want to help?'

She stared at him.

'Sorry if I was horrible earlier,' he said, giving half a smile.

'OK. *Pace.* Peace.'

'Peace.' They fist-bumped and grinned at each other.

Tara was tugging at a clump of long grasses. 'If we clear away this stuff at the bottom of the mound, we might find an entrance here.'

'There could be treasure!' said David.

'You and treasure,' said Tara. 'Mind the nettles, cuz! Don't get stung... and – argh! – watch out for these gorse bushes, too. They look severely spiky.' She shivered, murmuring, 'It's like they're guarding something. Hiding secrets. Oh! Look at the sky!'

Grey-black clouds were rolling in, covering the sun. The wind blew cold.

'Let's sit here for a minute,' said Tara. 'I need to ask the Bronze Mirror what we should do...'

White mists swirled.

Came a whisper:

And now, time traveller twins,
with Simone, your kin,
your next task
in this quest begins.

Enter the mound –
Go underground,

A crack in time
Is there to be found.

Travel to a past era,
Full of strife, anger, fear.
In a circle of oaks,
Where the raven croaks,
She awaits you, the Seer,
Know your next task is near.

But, before the next full moon,
On a night with no stars,
Beware the warrior God:
Beware – Mars!

Fiery eyes – smouldering, threatening – glowered at them from out of the Mirror.

The image dissolved into a night-black mist.

'He was in my dream,' whispered Tara. 'My nightmare.'

Simone trembled. 'What – what does this mean?'

Tara took a breath. 'The portal is opening – our second task begins.'

Simone clung onto her cousin's arm.

'We must be brave, cuz,' said Tara.

'*Si.* Yes. But—'

'This quest is more important than anything,' said David.

'I know – the planet is warming... But –' she frowned – 'what can we do?'

'Everyone can do something,' said Tara. 'Plant flowers for the bees...'

'Stop rivers being polluted,' added David.

'But why do we have to go back to the past?'

Tara shook her head. 'All I know is – we're being sent to a different time – to find the next crystal.'

'We have to fulfil this task, cuz,' said David. 'We agreed.'

'Each crystal will change the energy of the seas,' said Tara. 'Remember, the Goddess said, each will cleanse the oceans, the whole planet. And unless we find the crystals and cast them into the waters, life on Earth will be extinct.'

'But why are we here?' Simone looked around the clearing. 'Can't we raise money to save the forests? The animals? Why–?'

A sudden gust of wind sent leaves whirling. Lightning flashed. A rumble of thunder followed swiftly after. Heavy drops of rain began to fall.

Tara touched the Bronze Mirror.

Came the whisper:

Where the briars cling
Time spins,
Where the gorse grows,
Time flows.
Enter the mound,
Be unbound.

'The entrance must be here,' said Tara.

'To a tomb? A chamber?'

'*No!* Not a tomb? I can't—'

The rain was lashing down.

David stroked Bethan's ears. 'Find the entrance, little puppy.'

The spaniel raced along the edge of the mound, and disappeared around the other side.

They could hear her barking.

'The opening must be back there,' said David. 'Let's go.'

Bethan was pawing at the ground and whining.

'I can't see noth – anything,' said Simone, staring at the bright yellow gorse.

Bethan wriggled underneath and vanished.

Tara started to squeeze between the bushes. 'Ouch, sharp!'

David held the branches back. 'Careful, cuz. They're really spiky!'

Scrambling through the thicket, they found themselves in front of two huge standing stones; on top was a large, flat slab.

Severely awesome, Twin!

The portal must be here! I can feel it...

Simone started to shake. 'This feels so scary.'

'Definitely creepy.'

'Time to go in,' said Tara. 'Stay close together.'

'This could be a place to bury—' began David.

His sister glared at him.

Don't mention a burial mound, Twin. And keep Bethan on a tight leash.

'Er – bones – just animal bones. Dinosaur, maybe! Tyranno—'

Simone grimaced. 'Bones! Why are we going into a place with bones? I hate bones!'

The spaniel nudged David's leg.

'We know you love bones, Bethan! Come on, Simone. You said you don't need protection...'

Twin!

Sorry! Delete that!

Holding up the Bronze Mirror, Tara stepped forward into the tomb. Dark, dank, musty. The beam from the Mirror flickered over rough earthen walls.

'No bats, cuz,' she called. 'Looks like a passage. The roof's low. Mind your head.'

David wrapped the leash around his wrist and followed her in.

'Can you shine the Mirror behind you, Twin? It's pretty gloomy.'

Simone hung behind. *I'll just go a little way in and stop. They won't notice.*

Ergh! It smells very bad...

She took a step and another. *Oh no! I can feel the earth pressing down on my head; the walls are closing in on me.*

'Let's go down to Caerleon,' she called as she tripped over some hard shapes. *These could be bones... I'm going back...*

She tried to turn but found she couldn't move. *My heart's pounding. I feel I'm on fire. It's like hot needles being stuck into my chest.*

'Tara – David – I – I can't move!'

'Breathe. In, hold, and out. You're panicking – it'll pass,' called Tara.

The Bronze Mirror began to swivel around in her hand.

Oh! What's happening? It hasn't done this before.

'Can you hold onto Bethan, Twin?' said Tara. 'She'll be tripping me up...'

The puppy was straining at the leash. What could she see? What could she smell?

As they moved further down the passage, the light from the Mirror grew brighter, stronger. Scattered over the earthen floor were tiny slivers of flint and pieces of bone.

David bent down to pick up some of the smaller bones. 'These could be rabbit; or lambs. Maybe wolves?'

'*Lupi?* Wolves? *No!*

'There won't be any wolves here now,' said Tara. 'That was thousands of years ago.'

As they moved slowly down the passage, Tara noticed the walls had been hollowed out. The roof became higher. Further along, it divided in two tunnels; one sloped downwards, going deeper underground.

'Who used this place? And what for?' asked David. 'Do you think it's an Iron Age burial mound? That would be so cool! We might even find treasure in here!'

Why did you have to say that, Twin?

'A burial mound! Dead people!' Simone held her head in her hands.

'If there are any dead people here, they can't hurt us now,' said Tara.

'They'll drag us down to Hell! *Spectres.* Ghosts! Spirits!' Simone collapsed onto the mud floor.

'Come on, cuz.' David tried to pull her up. 'Nothing is going to happen to you – I promise.'

'How can you promise?' she wailed. 'You don't know. None of us know. We're all going to die in here.'

A figure flitted past, brushed her arm. and disappeared into the wall.

'Oh! Something touched my arm!'

David mind-messaged his twin. *Look – a shape. Now it's vanished. Oh, severely spooky!*

The puppy whimpered softly.

David, don't say anything... And keep hold of Bethan.

Simone groaned. 'I feel... *male*... bad, sick...'

'We all need to be calm, cuz.'

'I don't want to stay in here,' Simone choked. 'I'm frightened.'

'We won't be harmed,' whispered Tara. 'Just wait a—'

Came the whisper:

Look into the Mirror...

Faces of men and women, wrinkled and

wounded, scarred and shrouded in swirling mists
drifted in, then melted away.

Here, see, the Silures... ancestors of the tribe...
'O Dio mio!' cried Simone.

From out of the walls came fingers, snatching at
the Mirror.

'Stop!' shouted Tara. 'You cannot take this from
me. I am the Guardian of the Bronze Mirror!'

'I didn't touch it!' shouted Simone.

'Not you. Can't you see them?' Tara sighed. *How
I wish it wasn't just me that has this gift of seeing.
I feel so responsible for everyone, everything... It's
a lonely feeling. Especially now.*

'Something touched my cheek,' whispered David.

'Bats! Can we go now? *Per favore.* Please,' begged
Simone. 'I hate this place.'

Came the whisper:

Look again...

A shape appeared in the Mirror. A girl, her hands
outstretched.

'Can you see? A child is here,' Tara said. 'She's
pleading... She's asking for something... I've seen
her before.'

'What child?' Simone stared around wildly.

'We're listening.' whispered Tara.

A child's voice whispered:

*'Don't be afraid. I cannot hurt you. I'm beyond all
harm.*

I'm a spirit. A spirit from beyond the grave.
I dance on the tops of hills, and over rocks,

in the streams as they flow to the rivers,
Coming through the veil of death,
I dance, through the air, among the trees,
I dance over the seas.
I dance in the breeze,
in the rustling of the leaves.
I dance my song,
O my sad, sad song.'

Simone rocked backwards and forwards, groaning.

'Tell us your story,' said Tara.

The child's voice was soft and lilting.

'Outside our village I was. Fetching water from the stream. Above me, a big shadow came. I looked up. A tall man, wearing a helmet, was standing there. On the ground a shield. His cloak, red. Holding a spear, he was. The sun shone on it, bright and shiny. I smiled at him, this stranger. "Do you want water?" I asked. I offered my bowl. Then he took out a sword and stabbed me. Through my heart he stabbed me. I cried. I screamed. "Why?" His sword – red, it was, blood-red. Flowing...'

David swallowed.

'My spirit left my body. My people found me. They brought me here to lie with our ancestors. So many of us here now. Will there be more? I see him still. The soldier. Living near the river with many men. Marching. Making their swords sharp... The spirits say ships are coming, bringing more men.

Why are they here? – Are they coming to kill my people? Peace... we lived here in peace...'

'A Roman soldier killed her,' cried Simone. 'This is terrible.' She wiped tears from her checks.

Tara touched her arm. 'Remember, she's in her time.'

'Who are your people?' said David.

'The People of the Rocks, we are called - Silures. This is our home; this is our place; this is our land.' Her voice became shrill. *'They came here to steal, to kill, to destroy us. Help us – I beg you. Here I must stay until you have helped my people. Then I can go towards the light, to be with my ancestors...with the spirits, with the dreamers...'*

Her face began to fade.

'Stay!' said David. 'How can we help your people?'

Her voice grew fainter. 'The Seer... she will tell you... tell you all...'

The twins called after her. 'We'll help you.'

Bethan began to howl. The ground began to shake and rumble.

'Aiuto! Help!'

Tara reached towards Simone. 'Take my hand.'

The walls of the chamber began to crack and crumble. Pieces of the roof fell all around them. The puppy whimpered as David held her close. 'I'll protect you.'

'Oh no! There's a head – a – a – skull!'

A skeleton appeared, half in, half out of the wall; bones of hands, arms, legs.

A jaw full of teeth.

'O morte! O death!'

'The veil between our time and hers is disappearing,' whispered Tara.

'Like before, Twin?'

'This will be different. And more dangerous. We must be aware...'

'We're going to be buried alive.' Simone let go of Tara's hand and covered her head with her arms.

'The earth is going to smother me. We're all going to die here. *Aiuto!* Help me! Help...'

 **Chapter 3**

At the Hillfort

All was still. All was silent. Tara stretched out her arms and felt the earth beneath her. Firm. Solid. Above her, she saw an arc, a rainbow, spanning the sky.

Sitting up, she saw her twin. He was curled up next to a hedgerow, with Bethan sprawled on top of him.

Simone was lying flat in the shade of an oak tree. She called, 'Tara! David! Where are you?'

'Over here, cuz.'

'*Grazie!* We're out of that – that horrible mound. Do you think we're dead? Are we in Heaven?'

'If we are, then dogs live there, too!' laughed David as the puppy nuzzled his face. 'Stop that, Bethan! You were licking those old bones!'

Simone touched the grass. 'It's damp, but it isn't moving.' She propped herself up on her elbow. 'That – that – burial thing. Where is it? Has it been swallowed up?'

Tara waved her hand towards the mound. 'No. It's over there. Everything feels different, though. The air smells cleaner... fresher.'

Several large blue butterflies chased each other across the glade; one settled on an old tree stump covered with moss and ivy.

'Let's walk down to Caerleon before anything else happens to us,' said David, stroking the spaniel.

'*Si. Andiamo!* Let's go,' said Simone brushing leaves from her hair. 'I'll have to plait this again. That's strange. It feels shorter—'

'Now you're keen to see the Roman fortress!' David laughed. 'Let's eat our sandwiches first. Where are our backpacks? Can you see them, cuz? We can picnic here.'

There was silence, followed by a shriek. '*No! No!*'

'Simone?' Tara looked across. Her cousin had stood up and was staring at her clothes: a loose woollen tunic. She looked horrified.

'This is rough and baggy! Ergh! Terrible! Blue and yellow squares!'

Tara's tunic was wool too; dark green with red squares.

'My colours are better. But this tunic is so, er – scratchy, and it, it's...'

'Itchy?'

'*Si*. Yes.' She screwed up her face, 'C-cor–'

'Coarse,' sighed Tara.

At that moment, Bethan leapt up, bared her teeth, and growled. Into the clearing strode a man; short and swarthy, with wavy black hair and a straggly moustache.

'Here you are! Lying around! You should be inside the hillfort. It's too dangerous here – too near the Romans – they're down by the river. You, boy – Aled the blacksmith is waiting for you. Harnesses need repairing, axles and chariot rims. We need more swords, too.'

He scowled at them. 'Did you think you'd idle here after your journey from Llanmelin? The tribe sent you to help us, not to rest. Hurry! Or –' he waved over to the mound – 'we'll all be buried in there soon enough.'

Glancing at the girls, he pointed at Tara and said, 'You. 'You can grind the corn with Mariad. We need to feed the Roman hostages. Keep them healthy.'

He jabbed a finger at Simone. 'That can be your job. Find out everything they know about the governor's plans. That way, we can surprise them, ambush the legion, and defeat them for the last time.'

He turned and began walking back down the track. 'Come!'

Simone stared in horror at her cousins.

David mind-messaged his twin. *What shall we do?*

Follow him and see what happens...

Have you got the Mirror?

Tara felt for her bag; the Bronze Mirror was inside. *It's here. It's safe.*

Swivelling around, the man said, 'Since they captured Caratacus and took him to Rome, we've had to fight without our leader. But we will not be beaten! We are Silures!'

David nodded. 'Right.'

'Ah, Caratacus. Betrayed, he was.' Touching his dagger, he looked over to the burial mound. 'Revenge! Revenge!'

The spaniel growled and moved towards him.

David snatched her up. 'Bethan. Shush. Stop it.'

Glowering at them, the man shouted, 'Follow me.' He stared at the puppy, who was squirming in David's arms. 'What's that four-legged beast?'

Bethan bared her teeth at him.

'Ah, a hound. Bring it. It can hunt something.'

He stalked off.

'Who's Caratacus?' said David. 'What did he mean – a tribe sent us? And where's Llanmelin?'

'I don't know. Let's all say as little as possible.'

Simone was bewildered. 'What century are we in? And these clothes! Ugly woollen tunics.' She ran her fingers over the cloth. 'Worse than the Middle Ages!'

'Come on. We have to follow him,' said Tara.

'Why? He's horrible.' Simone stared wildly around. 'He talked about a river. Let's escape – in a coracle. Or go to the church for sanctuary, like we did in the Priory in Monmouth. That worked.'

'The church won't have been built yet,' said Tara. 'Besides, we promised the little girl...'

Simone folded her arms. '*You* promised.'

'We're a team. One for all and –'

'All for one,' said David. 'The Three Musketeers! And Bethan is the fourth!'

They raced along the track. The man was well ahead of them by now.

'That Caratacus sounds interesting, Twin. And I'll get to learn about chariots. Cool.'

'We've arrived in the middle of a war. The Goddess warned us. She said this task is going to be more dangerous than the last. We'll need to be aware of everything, and everyone.' She glanced back at Simone, who was panting and holding her side. And be careful what you say—'

'I could help them fight—' David replied.

'What? That's what I mean! Just keep *schtum*!'

'Er – right...'

Up and down deep ditches and ramparts, they clambered, making their way towards the hillfort.

Tara kept glancing to the left and right. *Who's watching us? Anyone could be hiding in these woods.* She felt a presence. *Does it wish us well? Or harm?*

A jackdaw cawed, shattering the silence. After they had passed a clump of birches, the track opened out into a clearing. They had arrived.

David gazed around the hillfort. 'Just like in those documentaries,' he whispered. 'See – there are the round houses – thatched roofs, made of timber and daub. Cool! Sheep, goats, cattle, chickens by the forge over there, pecking away. Weaving cloth... Maybe we're on a film set. I can smell something good cooking.'

Bethan sniffed. *Rabbit?*

The swarthy man was waiting for them by the fire. Wisps of smoke drifted up and over the trees. A young boy was over by the forge, handing some tools to the blacksmith.

'Edryn! Come!'

He ran over to them and smiled.

'The pair of you can work on the chariot over there. Help your father to repair the wheel.'

'Yes, Bryn. Hello.'

'Hi! My name's David.'

'I'm Edryn ap Aled. That's my father.' He pointed towards the blacksmith, who was hammering a long piece of iron on the anvil.

Bethan wagged her tail furiously at the boy and jumped up.

'Down, Bethan.'

'Is it a fox?'

The spaniel lifted up one ear, whined, and looked at David.

'She's a dog, a puppy.'

Edryn stoked her head. 'I can see she's special.'

I am. Can I have some food now?

'Have you been fighting the Romans?' the boy asked as they walked towards the forge.

Surprised, David blinked. 'Er – I have fought.' He was trying to stay as close to the truth as possible.

'What was it like?'

A woman with long, red-brown hair called to the girls. 'Come over here to the fire. Stir the soup. This is for the hostages. We have to keep them alive – and healthy, too.'

Where's the quern? thought Tara. *It must be here somewhere if I'm to grind the corn.*

'I have to grind—'

'Behind the forge. Mariad's there.' The old woman took a wooden ladle and spooned some soup into a large bowl.

Simone peered into the cauldron; dark green, bubbling liquid. The young girl grimaced.

'Are those nettles?'

'Yes. Go. The hostages are over there, inside that fenced area. Don't drop the bowl. Find out their plans. And remember – they're our enemies.'

Holding the bowl carefully, Simone walked towards the wooden stockade.

Ergh! Green mush. Nasty! she thought. *I like the zig-zag decoration on this bowl, though. So how am I going to persuade the hostages to tell me anything?*

Especially the governor's plans?

Two warriors stood guard at the gate; spears at the ready, daggers in their belts, their shields leaning against the fence.

'Er – hello,' said Simone. 'This is for the hostages.'

One grunted and opened the gate.

Slipping inside, she tripped and almost spilled the soup.

The soldiers were crouched down, throwing dice and laughing. One of them glanced up.

She smiled and nodded.

They'll think I'm a spy. How can I gain their trust? I'll speak Latin.

'*Salve!* Hello! *Estisne Romani?* Are you Romans?'

'Some of us are. Some of us aren't. We're all soldiers in the Second Augustan Legion.'

One stood up and took the bowl from her.

'I'm sorry you're prisoners here,' she said. 'Where are you from?'

The first hostage took a sip, spat it out, and

passed the soup to his friends. He shrugged.

Leaning against a wooden post he said, 'I'm Flavius. I come from North Africa. 'My people are Berbers; farmers there. It's a Roman Province now.'

I need to keep him talking, she thought.

'Why did you leave?'

He laughed. 'I joined the Roman army to see the world.'

There was bitterness in his voice.

'The world! Months marching through Iberia, up through Gaul. Gaul! Rain and mud! Mud and rain! Then, the legion is sent here – to Britannia!'

He looked through the open gate to where the Silures were going about their day; dyeing and weaving wool, milking the goats.

'We were told these people are savages, but they treat us well.' He looked her up and down. 'Why are you asking all these questions? You're not from this tribe?'

Here's my chance. 'I'm from Rome.'

'You're a prisoner too?' said Flavius.

'I – I am. My name's Simone.'

'Where do you come from? Where's your family from?'

'Egypt. My grandfather came from Rome with—'

She tried to remember the names of Roman generals. *Octavius? Marc Anthony? Is Caesar dead by now?*

'It must've been Octavius,' said Flavius.

'Exactly! Octavius!'

'How did you come here?'

The Romans were always invading places and making the people slaves. She sighed deeply.

'I'm a slave. I was captured by – er – and taken to Rome.'

'Yes, yes. But how did you get here – to Britannia? To Isca?' asked Flavius.

'First I was sent to – er – Ca—' She made a sad face, covered her mouth, and trembled.

'Camulodeum. You were in Camulodeum?' Flavius was astonished.

'You were there when Boudica attacked our town?' asked another soldier. 'And killed our people?'

I hope they won't ask me any more questions. I don't know anything about this.

Bowing her head, she wiped her eyes.

'You look too young to have been there.' Flavius narrowed his eyes.

'I – I – was just a child. A child slave.'

Who's Boudica? What happened at this Camulodeum place? Simone wondered.

She leaned forward, whispering, 'Can you help me to escape from here? Has your leader made any plans to get you back?'

One young soldier, who was gulping the soup, sneered, 'Our governor? Sextus Julius Frontius? He's more interested in building an aqueduct so that water flows in the right direction, than getting us back to the fort. His dreams are of lead pipes and drains!'

'Magnus! Do not speak of the governor like that,' snapped Flavius. 'His orders were to build the Roman Empire here. That's what he's doing.'

The legionary grinned. 'Ah, we all enjoy the games in our new amphitheatre, don't we?' He nudged his friend in the ribs. 'Julius Frontius had that built for us.'

Flavius frowned. 'Yes. And if we hadn't been hunting boar in these woods, we wouldn't have been caught. We could be there now, preparing for the games tomorrow.'

'Give me old Suetonius any day. Now he was a real general – slaughtering the Druids in the north. He knew how to enforce Roman rule. Kill 'em all!'

The youngest soldier shouted over to the guards.

'Oh, be quiet, Calvus!'

'I'm a prisoner, just like you.' Simone looked deeply unhappy. *I hope this works,* she thought. *And I feel like a prisoner...*

'When do you think the governor will attack the tribe here?'

'Difficult to say,' said Flavius. 'He wants to make Isca the biggest port in Britannia.' He took the bowl from Calvus. 'Although he could be leaving for Rome soon. The new governor of Britannia has arrived; Julius Agricola. That might make a difference.'

'But the rumour is he's going to the north first, to fight the tribes there,' said Magnus. 'So, we sit, and we wait.'

'And play *tali!*' laughed Calvus.

Flavius looked at Simone. 'Never fear. If our legion does attack, we'll take you with us.'

'Even though you're a girl, you're a Roman,' said Magnus.

Argh! Simone dug her nails into her palms. *The Romans didn't believe in equality. Men made the rules. Women stayed in the home. No wonder their Empire fell.* She managed a tight smile. 'That would be good. I'll be ready.'

Taking the empty bowl, she walked through the gate.

I've found out all this information. What do I do with it? Shall I tell anyone? I'm a Roman, after all...

Earlier, Tara had wandered past the roundhouses behind the forge. A girl with fiery red hair was grinding corn on a large round stone.

Is that Mariad? she wondered.

'Hello!' called Tara. 'Hello!'

The girl raised her head. 'You're from the hillfort by the sea.'

Does she mean the Severn estuary?

She walked over to where Mariad was moving the top stone backwards and forwards. 'Yes, I've come to help.'

'Thank you. But there's enough corn now.'

As the girl stood up, she glanced back over her shoulder to the edge of the clearing.

'I'm Mariad. What's your name?'

'Tara. My twin's called David. He's with Edryn now. And Simone – she's gone to take some food to the hostages – she's our cousin.'

Mariad brushed her hair back from her face. 'It's safer there.'

'Where?'

'At your hillfort. Llanmelin. Fewer Romans around there.' Mariad looked towards the trees again. 'So, you've been sent – to help this tribe.'

'Er – yes – you're not a Silures?'

'No. I'll just take this grain over to Bryony. Wait here.'

*What **was** she looking at?* Tara glanced around the clearing. An oak tree, uprooted by a storm was lying on its side.

Came a whisper:

Moss and ivy cling
To this fallen trunk with many rings.

Tara spun around. There, at the edge of the woods, was a circle of oaks. And a rowan tree. A shiver ran through her.

You have been given a task,
The Seer knows – Come. Ask.

Tara whirled around. *Who's speaking to me? Where's this voice coming from? Is it the Bronze*

Mirror?

David was at the blacksmith's forge. Bethan was gnawing on a bone. Simone was walking away from the stockade, frowning.

Puzzled, Tara scanned the glade again.

Look towards the circle,
Look towards the oaks...

A woman was sitting under the rowan tree.

Tara was startled. *She wasn't there just now. I saw her in my dream... Is she a friend – or—?*

Mariad appeared and took Tara's arm. 'The Seer wishes to speak with you.'

The rowan tree, tree of enchantment. Bright red berries, warding off evil spirits...

Keeping the bag close to her heart, she held the Bronze Mirror tightly.

Protect me, she thought, as she walked towards the sacred grove.

Chapter 4

The Seer

Sitting cross-legged on the ground was a woman with dark red-brown hair down to her waist. Her face was lined, her skin sun-browned.

She was wearing a tunic of many colours: indigo, blue, green, red, golden yellow. Loosely wrapped around her was a linen cloak, pinned with a brooch. Around her neck was a golden torc. Next to her, thrust into the earth, was a wooden staff.

The Seer was murmuring.

Spells? Incantations? Tara noticed the torc.

Eight twists of gold. Stunning! She must be one of the Dreamers. A Druid. A woman of power. For good? Or for—?

'We have been waiting...' whispered the Seer. 'Waiting for the travellers to come, from another time, from another world; a world where humans have lost their way. Your Earth is crying... I feel it, I hear it.'

Half closing her eyes, she swayed slightly.

'The veil has parted. To this place you have been sent – from many years in the future you have been sent. Sent by the Goddess. Why? To complete a task. To fulfil a quest. This you know, O Guardian of the Bronze Mirror. Great responsibility has been given to you.'

She narrowed her eyes and stared at Tara's bag.

Tara clasped the Bronze Mirror tightly to her. *I must be calm...*

'Here,' continued the Seer, 'this tribe is in grave danger from the soldiers, from the power and might of the Roman Empire. The warriors here wish to attack the fortress below.' She paused.

'Even now, they prepare for battle. Painting their faces, decorating their arms, braiding their hair, as is the custom. Blood must not be shed. Our gods, our goddesses, have spoken. You are here to bring an end to these battles. This you must do.'

'But how?'

'There are ways; many ways...' said the Seer. 'A vision I have seen. In time, the seas will rise, the air will become impure. Spring will come, yet no birds will sing, no bees will collect pollen, gradually all Life on this planet will die... But this, O warrior, you can change. You can save your world. But this task is mighty.'

A wren flew onto the hazelwood staff, glanced at the Seer, then darted off.

Her eyes. Like a panther, watching, waiting – ready to pounce? A woman to be wary of? I must show no fear, thought Tara.

'You think all is peaceful here.' Leaning back, the Seer gestured towards the clearing.

Children were chasing each other with twigs; a woman tossed kindling onto the fire. Some of the tribe were using plants to dye wool; others were spinning flax. In an enclosure, a large sow lay on her side, her piglets feeding.

'Now look over there...'

Tara turned towards the forge. A group of men and women were sharpening their swords.

'They are preparing to fight.'

Tara was horrified. 'But how can I – how can we – stop this?'

'By choosing each step of the path wisely. By fulfilling your next task. Or – more blood will be shed. To the spirit world I journeyed. This I was shown.'

The Seer closed her eyes and was silent.

'When will—?'

'Wait,' said Mariad. 'She's listening to the spirits.'

'Who is she?' murmured Tara.

'The daughter of a Druid. When she was a child, the Romans crossed to Mona, an island in the north, and killed her people. The Druids called down curses upon them. Her own grandmother cursed them. "May they never prosper unto their children's children. May their cities burn and their empire fall."' She paused. 'The Druids were killed in their sacred grove. Only her mother escaped. Her daughter was born later with the gift.'

'The gift?'

'The gift of seeing. The Seer now travels from tribe to tribe, helping the people, foretelling events, guiding them.' She smiled 'I am her granddaughter.'

The Seer stirred. 'Mariad. Bring the boy and girl here. Edryn, too. It is time.'

At the forge, Aled the blacksmith was making another sword. Next to him lay several chariot wheels. He stopped to wipe the sweat from his brow.

Edryn was showing David a wheel. 'Here's the broken bit, the lynch pin. That part needs repairing. Can you see?'

'Er – yes.' David was gazing at a pile of brooches, torcs and objects lying in a pile on the ground. Picking up a bronze horse, he said, 'Wow! This is fantastic!'

His new friend smiled. 'Thank you. I put on the red enamelling and the spirals, too. But now we need more weapons to fight the Romans. Perhaps we'll be going into battle soon. Look over there, by the woods. Our chariots and horses are ready.'

'You two, work more, talk less!' called the blacksmith. 'You'll not be making any bronze horses for a while, Edryn. Daggers and swords are what we need now. And repair those wheels!'

Looking up to the sky, he said, 'Twenty-five years of war there's been. Twenty-five years. We must defeat these invaders. Send them back to Rome. Make an end of it.'

He continued to hammer the sword blade with strong, powerful blows. Strike by strike, the iron was wielded into shape. David stared at the blacksmith's muscled shoulders. *Who'd want to fight him?*

Edryn examined the lynch pin. 'To ride in a chariot into battle – that'd be exciting.' His eyes shone. 'Such stories I'd tell around the fire to our children and grandchildren.'

If you live, thought David. Aloud he said, 'You're a storyteller?'

'I am. My name, Edryn, means a teller of myths and legends; a bard. I make up songs and poems.'

David couldn't stop himself. 'The Romans are the most powerful army ever,' he blurted out. 'No one has ever defeated them. Couldn't you live at peace with them – until things change? Until they leave? If you fight them, they'll destroy your tribe. You'll be crushed.'

Edryn was shocked. 'Shush! Don't let anyone hear you say that!'

Aled glared at the boys.

'Edryn! Come!' Mariad called. 'The Seer wants to speak to you in the sacred grove, and' – she pointed to David – 'that boy, too. Quickly!'

Edryn looked at his father.

Aled nodded. 'Go!'

'Come on, Bethan. Leave your bone.'

They raced towards the trees.

'Who's the Seer?' said David.

Geese hissed and ducks waddled out of their way.

'She's a Druid. And Mariad's grandmother. They're staying here with our tribe until the next new moon. She sees the future. She's one of the dreamers. Our gods, our goddesses, the spirits, reveal their secrets to her.'

Is she part of our task? wondered David.

Simone was walking back towards the fire. *Walk tall, shoulders back.* 'Even though I am a girl! Argh! I'll show them!'

Mariad was calling her. 'Simone! Hello! I'm Mariad. Come. My grandmother will speak with you.'

Simone was wary. 'Why? What about?'

Grasping her arm, Mariad began pulling her towards the oaks. 'The task! She'll tell us what we have to do. We need to go to the sacred grove. Now!'

Simone threw herself down between the twins. 'I've met the hostages...'

'Tell us later, cuz,' said David.

The young girl sighed. Then she stood up and brushed some grass from her tunic.

'Just sit down,' hissed Tara.

Bethan lay with her head on David's lap and went to sleep.

Hey Twin! David mind-messaged his sister. *What's the story here?*

We've been sent here to stop a battle between the Silures and the Romans.

Sounds a bit – er, tricky.

Minutes passed.

The Seer breathed deeply, opened her eyes, and slowly gazed around the five. Then she scanned Simone: her head, face, eyes, body. The girl from Rome looked away and started to pick some daisies.

She's checking her aura, thought Tara. *Noting her strengths and her weaknesses.*

'Who is this woman?' Simone whispered. 'Why are we here?'

'Listen,' said Tara. 'We're about to find out.'

The Seer sighed deeply.

'Through time, through space, you have travelled; a quest to fulfil, a task to complete. Your World to save.'

A blue-black shadow flew across the glade.

A raven. Is that an omen? Tara wondered.

'First, granddaughter, tell of the struggle of the tribes, of the people of this island, Britannia.'

Mariad turned to face the trio. 'For decades, the Iceni in the East, and many of our tribes, resisted the Roman invaders. Some have been crushed brutally, others have yielded; paid taxes to Rome, learnt their language, followed their customs. For years, the Silures refused to give up the fight, even though many of their warriors were killed. Now the Roman army has settled here. Their fortress, they call Isca, is below. More soldiers continue to arrive over land, and at their new port here.'

Edryn looked fierce and sad at the same time.

'What can we do to help?' said David.

'I don't see how we can,' began Simone.

The Seer stared deep into the young girl's eyes. 'The time is here. The time is now. Only one path can be taken. Only one choice can be made. Choose.'

Simone trembled. *Choose? What does she mean? Choose what?*

Taking out a folded piece of cloth from beneath her cloak, the Seer placed it on the ground.

A magpie chattered in a gnarled old oak. Tara looked around.

Is there another? she wondered. *No... One for sorrow... Again.*

The Seer was speaking. 'Your second task will now be revealed.'

The twins exchanged glances.

'An hour before the sun rises, go through these woods, down to the fortress.' She paused. 'A precious object, a talisman, is hidden there. Search for it. Bring it to me. Only then will the Silures be safe from the Roman soldiers.'

Simone looked desperately at the twins while Tara touched her bag and felt the outline of the Mirror.

The Seer unwrapped the cloth. Four iron nails lay there; long, thin, sharp.

Puzzled, the trio stared at them.

'These nails were made by the grandfather of Aled, now charged with powerful energy; energy from our gods and goddesses, when the moon was new.'

'Spells. She means spells,' whispered Simone. 'Oh no! She's a witch!'

She made a move to get up.

Tara gripped her arm. 'Stay, cuz. This is our

task. We must find the talisman.'

'And help the tribe,' added David. 'This is important.'

The Seer's face began to change. Her cheeks hollowed; her voice deepened.

'May the energy from these nails protect this tribe from all harm. To these travellers; these who have been sent through time, through space, this is the message: Around the Roman fortress, place these nails. At each gate. North, south, east, west. Bury them deeply. A circle, a powerful force, will be created. Say these words: "May the energy in this nail contain these soldiers of Rome within. May the energy in this nail protect the Silures." Repeat these words.'

While Mariad and Edryn were saying the words, Simone stared in terror at her cousins.

'I – I can't say those words. I—'

'Why not?' said David.

'It's a spell. And it's against the Romans.'

'It's to stop more bloodshed. If we do this, there won't be any more battles.' He glared at his cousin. 'Look around. Do you want these children to die? For the tribe to be destroyed?'

Simone looked away. '*No!* Of course not.'

'So – let's remember the words,' said David.

'But—'

'But nothing!' he snapped.

The Seer shuddered, breathing deeply.

David mind-messaged his twin. *What happened?*

A spirit of the Druids had entered her. Look. Now she is as she was before.

Spooky. Ah – she's looking at you, Tara.

'These four nails must be kept in your bag, with the Bronze Mirror,' said the Seer.

Looking sternly at Simone, she said, 'For their power to work, for the legion to be held inside the fortress, all four nails must be buried in a circle; south, west, north and east. The Romans must not attack this tribe.'

Simone clasped and unclasped her hands.

David cleared his throat. 'About this, er – object – this talisman we must find. What is it, exactly? Big, small? How will we find it?'

'You will be told.' The Seer's eyelids flickered. 'Leave the animal here until your return.'

Bethan started whining.

'But—'

'I have spoken.'

Shadows lengthened. Jackdaws were gathering in the tops of trees. *Caw! Caw!* they croaked.

The trio stood away from the roundhouses at the edge of the woods.

'She's a witch! I know she is. Did you see how her face changed? She's a very scary woman,' said

Simone. 'Why do we have to do what she tells us? And – I'm a Roman.'

David was astonished. 'What? You only live there. Your father's Egyptian, and your mother was born here, in Wales. Practically a Silures! The fact you live in Italy in the 21st century isn't anything to do with this.'

His cousin was furious. 'What do you know?'

'It's obvious!'

He knelt to stroke the puppy. 'I don't want to leave you here with the blacksmith. But you'll have lots of bones to eat; deer, goat, sheep...'

Bethan stretched out her front legs and looked up at David.

Bones sound good. But do I have to stay with that tall, angry man? And that scary woman?

Tara sighed. 'Cuz, we've been sent here to stop the tribe being killed. What's your problem?'

Simone kicked at a tuft of grass. 'Not a problem...'

'Whatever you are feeling – you too, David – just lose it... anger, fear, resentment... Get rid of it. We must be positive about this task. Otherwise it's not going to work. And we have to find the talisman.'

Simone shrugged. 'Maybe the Silures weren't killed anyway. Maybe they'll survive whether we find this thing – this talisman – or not. Maybe our being here doesn't make any difference.'

She's sabotaging the task before it's even begun. David mind-messaged his twin. *Talk to her. Make her see we are here to do something important. More important than her feelings.*

You tell her, Tara replied. *Tell her about what the Romans did here in Britain.*

David took a deep breath.

'Simone – the Romans invaded, took lands, stole the minerals – gold and silver – killed thousands – and they stayed and ruled for four hundred years.'

'*Si* – I know all that.'

David looked confused. 'We get very upset when that happens in our world – in the 21st century – when a country invades another. Why do you think it was OK two thousand years ago?'

'The hostages told me about one tribe – they killed lots of Romans. In Cam – somewhere...'

'That was the Iceni. Boudica was Queen of the Iceni tribe. The Romans stole her lands and flogged her in front of everyone. It was terrible. She fought back, resisted them. Fought for justice. She's a hero,' said David. His face was fiery. 'So you think it's alright to invade a country, kill thousands of people, make them follow your rules, steal their land...?'

Simone opened her mouth to speak. 'I—'

'Let's all calm down. You don't really believe that, cuz...'

'I—'

'Tell us, Simone,' said David.

'Right,' said Tara, stamping her foot. '*Schtum*, both of you! I've had enough. We're here to help this tribe. That's our task. We made a pact, a promise. And we'll keep it. The three of us. We'll complete this task. We'll fulfil the quest. All of us.'

David frowned. 'We never ever break a pact, cuz. It's sacred.'

At that moment, Tara saw an image. A crystal; pale purple, long, pointed.

It appeared, then vanished. *I dreamt this...* she thought. *I saw this...*

David had been speaking. 'So, we'll find a way to get into the fortress and discover this talisman. Then we get back here, hand it over to the Seer, travel back to the 21st century. Task completed.' He patted the spaniel. 'I hope in time for bara brith!'

Simone threw an angry look at him. 'Food! *Pah!* You only ever think about your stomach.'

'What's really the matter, cuz?' said Tara.

Her cousin shrugged. 'The hostages – they're all Roman; part of the Empire, anyway. Flavius is from North Africa.' She gulped. 'And the Seer, she scares me. She sees into your mind. She knows all your secrets. She does.' Scrunching up her face, she said, 'I can feel it.'

'All we have to do is find the talisman,' said David. 'We don't have to get caught up in anything else. Alright?'

She shrugged her shoulders. '*Si.* Yes.'

'Then the plan is, we stay here tonight, and before dawn we'll go down to the fortress with

Mariad and Edryn,' said David.

'Put a nail at each gate. Say the words,' said Tara. 'And search for the talisman.'

'How will we know what it is?' said Simone. 'Or where it is?'

'We'll be told...' said Tara. 'The Bronze Mirror will tell us.'

Twin, let's keep an eye on Simone. She's...

Wobbly?

Reluctant...

The sun had slipped behind the hills in the west. Reds, yellows, oranges blazed, followed by slivers of purple, light grey, and night-darkness.

Every member of the tribe was sitting around the fire. A goat was being roasted on a spit. Aled picked up a large iron tankard, drank, and passed it around the circle. Each took a sip. Simone put it near her lips, pretended to drink, and passed it to Tara.

Later, when the moon had risen, Mariad led the trio into a small roundhouse and left them lighted candles.

'Goodnight. I'll come for you an hour before dawn.'

Looking around, Simone grimaced. 'I suppose we have to sleep on this earth floor.'

David picked up an animal hide and settled down underneath, with Bethan.

'This is cosy. OK, it smells of deer...'

'Ugh!' Simone found a rush mattress and threw herself on it.

As she drifted off to sleep, Tara clasped the bag to her heart; feeling the hard outline of the Bronze Mirror. Images flittered through her mind: horses rearing up; a chariot; crowds of people shouting, screaming.

What is the talisman? Where is it hidden? Will we find it?

Chapter 5

The First Riddle

Mariad led the way through the woods. In darkness or in light, she knew every bend of this steep track.

Behind her, Tara watched where she placed each foot. Rustling sounds came from all around. *Hedgehogs, badgers, dormice?* she wondered.

Simone was swishing at ferns with a branch.

'Cuz, you said the Roman Governor doesn't want to attack the Silures?'

'That's what Flavius told me,' said Simone in a flat voice. 'I don't know why we're doing this.'

'For peace,' said Mariad.

David was worrying about Bethan. He hadn't wanted to leave her with Aled at the forge. *She was chewing a large bone when we left,* he thought. *I guess she'll be happy there for a few hours.*

'Tell us about Caratacus,' he said as they stopped to let some badgers snuffle across the path.

'Ah, Caratacus,' sighed Edryn. 'A brave warrior. After his tribe had been crushed, he led us against the Romans. Then there was his final battle – over towards the west.'

'He was killed?'

'No – betrayed. He fled north to find safety. But Queen Cartimandua handed him over to our enemies. Paraded in Rome before the Emperor Claudius, he was; a trophy. We heard he gave such a powerful speech the emperor pardoned him. He's there still. But his spirit's here.' He swallowed hard. 'So we resisted, we kept fighting.'

Mariad nodded. 'Like Boudica. But times change...'

Tara mind-messaged her twin. *I hope that the Seer's magic works. And when we bury these nails, they'll keep the soldiers inside the fortress. No more bloodshed. And we can search for the talisman.*

Morning mists were rising from the river as they arrived at the edge of the woods. Across the meadow, they could see the outline of the fortress.

'Let's sit here, behind these trees, so no one will see us,' said Mariad.

Taking the piece of linen from her bag, Tara unwrapped it and placed the nails on the ground.

'What energy!' said Edryn.

'Awesome!'

Rusty old nails, thought Simone.

'How about Edryn and I take two and bury them by two of the gates?' said David.

'And we'll take two,' said Tara. 'Agreed?'

'Agreed.'

Four heads nodded. Simone stared straight ahead.

David mind-messaged his twin. *Is our cuz alright?*

I'm not sure. Mariad and I will keep her with us.

Edryn picked up a stick and drew a rough outline on the earth. 'This is how the fortress is laid out.' He made a cross. 'We're here. There's the river.' He picked up a large, round stone, and put it down. 'That's the amphitheatre.'

David was surprised. 'It's outside the fortress?'

'Yes, and –' Edryn placed four smaller stones to mark south, north, east and west – 'these are the gates.'

Taking some twigs, he placed them inside the fort. 'Here are the barracks. The headquarters and the governor's residence are right in the middle. The baths are opposite. The granaries—'

Simone murmured, 'Always the same.'

'What do you mean?' said David.

She shrugged. 'They build their forts exactly the same, everywhere they go.'

Mariad frowned at her as Edryn continued. 'And the Temple of Diana is over here, near the river.'

'How do you know all this?' asked Tara.

'The tribe's been watching them for years – ever since they came here.'

Turning to the boys, Mariad said, 'If you bury the nails by the south gate and then the west, we'll go around to the north, and finally the east.'

'East,' muttered Simone.

'And then the circle will be completed,' said David.

'Is everyone agreed?' asked Tara, glancing at her cousin.

Simone didn't answer. She clasped both hands around her knees and stared at the fortress.

Tara handed one nail to Edyrn and one to her twin. 'Go now. Make for the south gate, over there. Then the west, and come back here.'

'We'll skirt around you and go to the north gate,' said Mariad. 'Then around to the East Gate.'

'It'd be quicker if you went to the East Gate first,' said Simone.

'But it has to be clockwise,' said Tara.

'And,' said Edryn, 'we mustn't forget to say the words.'

'We really mustn't,' said Simone.

'Hey, cuz, what is the matter?' said David.

'*Niente.* Nothing at all.'

There was silence.

'Say what you're thinking. Otherwise we can't do this, cuz,' said Tara.

'You don't need me.'

'We **do** need you, Simone,' said Tara. 'After we've buried the nails, we'll be told where to find the talisman. Then we'll search for it. This task needs all of us.'

'Hmmm.'

Tara sat back on her heels. 'Any anger or resentment you've got – it'll get in the way.'

'You keep saying that,' said Simone.

'It's true.'

Mariad and Edryn exchanged puzzled looks.

'How about we sit quietly for a few minutes?' said Tara.

'*Si.* Yes. If you want.'

Simone could ruin everything, Twin. Do something!

Tara sighed. 'There's something we do before beginning a task. It clears our minds, helps us focus. We close our eyes, breathe in, count to three. Hold for two counts, and out for five.'

'It helps us get rid of any bad moods,' said David.

Twin!

'I like this idea,' said Mariad, smiling. 'Before battle, we pray to our gods, our goddesses.'

They sat on the ground, closed their eyes, and took in long, deep breaths.

Several minutes passed.

None of them saw two deer standing nearby, heads up, ears twitching, staring at them. As David yawned and stretched, the animals turned and fled into the woods, flashing their white tails.

'So – this talisman – where is it?' said Simone.

'We'll be told,' said Tara. 'I guess after the nails are buried.'

'Maybe it'll be a code,' said David. 'Or a sign.'

Tara looked around at the faces. 'I'll ask now.' She took the Bronze Mirror out of her bag.

A whisper came:

Remain aware! Never despair!
What you seek is rare;
Made for a warrior's hand,
To make a stand; to protect this land.

A perilous path a warrior trod.
To fight the wrath of the Roman god.
Remain aware! Never despair!
As you seek and search for that which is rare.

David was the first to speak. 'A riddle.'

'That which is rare,' said Tara.

'Made for a warrior's hand,' said Edryn. 'A sword?'

'Or a dagger?' said David.

'*Si.* Yes. Made for a man's hand.'

'Our warriors are men and women,' said Mariad.

'Rare. How can it be rare?' said Simone. 'The Romans have lots of swords.'

'My father's swords are unique,' said Edryn. 'Each one.' He turned to David. 'Sometimes, he lets me decorate the scabbards.'

'Perhaps the talisman is a special sword – a magic sword,' said Tara.

'One made for a warrior who fought against the Romans,' said Mariad.

'Against their god of war.' David shivered. 'Mars.'

Tara placed the Bronze Mirror back into her bag. 'Perhaps after we've buried the nails, we'll be told the second riddle.'

David leapt up. 'Let's go now. Look at the sky. It's getting lighter. We don't want to get caught and thrown into a Roman dungeon. What a nightmare that would be!'

'You go first,' said Tara. 'We'll wait a few minutes, then head for the river and the north gate.'

She gazed across to the fortress. Hovering high above it was a hawk. *All seeing,* she thought.

'Let's meet back here afterwards,' said Mariad. 'We'll have the cover of these woods.'

The boys crawled along the ditches by the side of the fortress, and reached the South Gate. Peering around, they noticed some legionaries standing near a circular oven. It was set into the ramparts.

A dark-haired young soldier was giving orders.

'Hurry up! Cook us some barley cakes. We've got drills soon. No one can live on these measly rations.'

'Yes, Gaius Tarquin Livinius.'

Two oxen were pulling a loaded cart towards the gate. As they struggled along the muddy track, a soldier tugged at the yoke.

'Faster! Move faster!' he shouted.

'That cart is perfect cover,' said David. 'If we walk behind it with our heads down, no one will see us. Then we can get close to the gate entrance.'

'Maybe we should wait until later? The soldiers will be at their drills then.'

'Let's seize the day, Edryn! Oh, I'm buzzing! Follow me!'

Running across the track, he slid behind the cart and bowed his head.

His friend raced to join him.

The oxen plodded on. Before the entrance, the boys jumped down into a deep ditch. Neither of the guards saw or heard them.

Flattening himself against the slope, David looked up. A pair of old leather boots and the bottom of a javelin were all he could see.

He strained to hear what they were saying.

'So, three days of games to honour Apollo.'

'A change from parading and drills.'

'And digging ditches for drainage pipes!'

The wheels of the cart squeaked to a halt.

'*Salve.* Good day to you!'

'Password?' asked the guard.

'Remus.'

'Go along the via principalis and around to the

workshops. As usual.'

The man grunted. The cart turned into the main street.

David scrambled further up to the top of the ditch.

Edryn tugged at his tunic. 'Be careful.'

'We need to hear what's happening,' whispered his friend.

'As we were saying,' said a guard, 'these Games – they won't be as good as the Circus Maximus.'

'Nothing's better than Rome! But there'll be enough gladiators and wild animals fighting for their lives.'

'Hear about that gladiator – Sca—?'

'Scorpio? He was killed this year.'

'Yes. Leaning back round a bend. What a disaster!'

'He was the best chariot racer ever. Unbelievable!'

'Four horses at full gallop crashing into the barrier. What a spectacle that must've been! Lots of blood!'

'Wish I'd seen it. Totally mangled—'

'Hey! That's a cold wind from the river.'

'Let's shelter back here.'

'Linus Paulinus will be checking on us...'

The guards stepped away from the entrance.

David waited for a minute. 'Bury the nail now,' he whispered, pressing himself against the wall. 'Quickly!'

Footsteps. The soldiers were coming back.

'They say that someone had put a curse on Scorpio so he'd lose. Thousands of *denarii!*'

'Is that right? Curses!' The soldier spat. 'They come back on you. Mark my words.'

Having dug a small hole, Edryn pushed the nail into the earth; he whispered the spell.

'Did you just hear something?' asked a guard.

'I'll look.'

The boys held their breath.

Leaning over the ditch, the soldier looked left and right. 'Nothing! It's still a bit misty. Maybe it was a fox.'

'Time to report to headquarters and...'

Their voices drifted away.

'Let's go now, before they come back,' muttered David.

'To the West Gate.'

As they raced along the bottom of the ditch, they caught a glimpse of Tara and Mariad near the riverbank. But there was no sign of Simone. Where was she?

The mist had lifted. Gulls were wheeling above the river as Mariad stood up. 'Let's go now,' she said.

Simone was drawing patterns in the earth with

a stick. 'You two go. I'll wait here.' She reached over to take Tara's bag. 'I'll look after the Bronze Mirror, keep it safe.'

Tara clutched the bag. 'No, cuz. I'm its Guardian. Only I can look after it. You know that.'

Simone scowled. 'I really don't care.'

'What **is** the matter?'

'I don't want to do this!' Simone banged the stick so hard on the ground that it broke.

Tara sighed. *Time to have this out.*

'Simone. We're a team. And we all promised—'

Throwing the bits of stick into some bushes, her cousin snapped, 'You just don't care about me. I've been dumped here by my parents for weeks, maybe months. There's nothing to do and nowhere to go. No shops. No fun.'

Tara groaned.

'And I had to sleep under a thing – smelly, nasty skin of some animal – ugh! Well, I didn't sleep. And I had to eat a goat! A goat! Tough and ch – er – chewy... Just horrible. And I'm a Roman. You want me to betray my own people.'

Why did she have to say that?

Mariad was shocked. 'You're a Roman?'

'No. This is a misunderstanding. Isn't it?' Tara glared at her cousin.

'Hmm.'

'Her mother's my aunt. Aunt Fay. She was born near here. She comes from here. Up the hill...'

'A Silures?'

'Er – yes.' *I hope this isn't a lie. Anyway, it could be true...*

Simone smirked. 'Actually, my father is from Egypt. A completely different tribe.'

Mariad looked confused.

I want to strangle my cousin... But let that thought go... Breathe deeply. Don't be affected by her words, her emotions. They're hers, not mine. What does Nanny Lita always say? Take no notice... Stay calm...

'Yes, Egypt,' said Tara. 'Remember – the Romans conquered it. Didn't they, Simone? Remember Cleopatra?'

Mariad was impressed. 'You belong to the tribe of the great woman pharaoh? We learnt of her from the traders. Strong, fearless. A warrior!'

Startled, Simone said, 'Er – I am. I'm related to Cleopatra. Oh, yes...'

'A direct descendant,' said Tara. *And probably an exact reincarnation!*

'So, Simone, your country, Egypt, was invaded, your people were made slaves, and all the wealth was taken to Rome. You must know exactly how we feel.'

Simone flinched, then nodded.

'Good, now that's all sorted, it's time for us to bury the nail. Isn't it, cuz?'

'*Sí.* Yes...'

Tara picked up the third nail and handed it to Mariad. 'This one is for the North Gate.'

Making her voice light, she said, 'Cuz, do you remember the words to say?'

Simone crossed her fingers behind her back. '*Si.* Yes.'

'Then let's you and I bury the fourth nail at the East Gate.'

Simone stretched out her hand and took the nail. 'I want to bury this one myself. I'll meet you back here. I can run fast.'

'Er – we—'

But she'd already set off towards the east.

'Simone – that's the wrong way,' called Tara. 'You need to go all the way around the fortress – We have to go clockwise.'

'Ah – yes.' Simone switched directions.

'But—'

'I'll be quick.'

Shaking her head, Tara thought, *Why is she acting like this?*

'Bury it on the left of the East Gate. Say the words,' called Mariad after her as Simone raced towards the riverbank. 'If you get caught, say nothing. Or make up a story.'

'*Va bene.* Alright.'

'Come back soon. We need to hear the second riddle,' said Tara as her cousin disappeared amongst a clump of birches.

'Why is she going off on her own?' asked Mariad.

Tara shrugged. 'I really don't know.'

The boys stared up at the two arches. The West Gate. A helmeted figure holding a spear was standing in front of a shield; a chariot with two horses was behind.

'That's Mars, their warrior god,' said Edryn. 'But where are the guards?'

'Maybe they're preparing for the games,' said David. 'Let's bury this nail quickly and go.'

Scooping out some earth, he pushed the nail into the hole. He'd finished whispering the words when he heard the chink of armour behind them.

Who's this? He spun around.

The young soldier who'd been giving orders earlier, stood staring at them.

Those stick-out ears. Who do they remind me of? thought David. He smiled broadly. '*Salve!* Good day!'

Edryn was rigid. He kept his eyes on the ground.

'What are you doing?'

'Here? Ah, my sandal fell off. I was mending it,' said David.

'Where have you come from? Burrium?'

'Yes – er – Burri-er-um. That's right. We've been sent to collect some – er – oil, fish sauce,' *What else do they eat?* 'and olives...'

The legionary looked them up and down.

'Names? What are your names?'

'I am Davidus, and this is my brother, Eddidus.'

'From?'

'Castra Salsoviensia,' said David, trying not to laugh.

Tarquin looked puzzled. 'I don't know where—' He puffed out his chest. 'So,' he stared at their muddy tunics, 'you are slaves. Runaway slaves.'

'Slaves? Us? No!' said David. 'Our father is Antonio Septimus Cassio. Governor of one of the eastern provinces. You'll have heard of him. He's famous. Like I said, Castra Sal – Salsoviensia. That was before he retired and came here – to Britannia. Now he's a – a merchant. He trades in tin, gold, pottery, figs, olives – anything, really. From Ostia to – er – here – Isca.' He laughed. 'Did you see that ox slipping into a ditch over there? That's why we look like this. We need to jump in the baths! Or even the river! Eh, Eddidus?'

His friend was trying not tremble.

The young soldier pulled back his shoulders. 'My name is Gaius Tarquin Livinius.' He waved towards a group of young soldiers. 'I'm in charge of those soldiers over there. I've a very important position.'

David looked serious and nodded.

Those eyes– they're familiar. He brushed the mud off his tunic. *I need to think of a way out of this – and quickly.*

'We haven't been in Britannia long. We've been

sent here – to Isca – to take some pottery back to our father – in – er – Burr – Burrium,' said David.

'Why are you taking it back?' Tarquin looked puzzled.

'Damaged... they were damaged in transit. Rejected goods. Past their sell-by date. Refund required...'

Are these the right words for this century? Maybe not...

David added, 'We have to go to the quay now, to meet Octavius Crispus Maximus.' He put his hand on his chest and said, 'We must do our best for the Empire.'

Tarquin narrowed his eyes. 'Do you boys know why we are here in Isca?' He looked across to the hills beyond the river. 'To find gold in the west, to achieve glory for the Emperor. Then we'll return to Rome triumphant. Victorious! March through the Forum. Oh, how magnificent that will be...' His eyes glazed over; he lowered his voice. 'I'll be an *optimo* soon, then a centurion – after that a general. The Second Augustan Legion will be marching behind me. The crowds will be cheering. Emperor Vespasian will reward me with gold, silver. I'll build a villa...'

David fixed a smile on his face. *He's living in a fantasy world.*

'You were born in Rome? You're a Roman citizen. That's awe – er – excellent.'

Tarquin hesitated. 'I was born in Sicily. And I

always wanted to be a Roman citizen. I felt I belonged to Rome. I've been a soldier, an auxiliary, for five years now. In two decades, I'll receive a bronze diploma with a pension, too. But soon I'll be commanding this legion.'

'Cool! Er – very good.'

Sounds of swords clashing, and orders being given, drifted across from the amphitheatre.

Tarquin leaned forward. 'Have you heard the latest news? Perhaps from your father?'

What does he mean? David put on a knowing expression. 'Well—'

'There's a rumour. Now that Julius Agricola, the new governor, has arrived in Britannia, several cohorts from this legion may be ordered to march north soon, to Caledonia, to fight against those –' he shuddered – 'savages. They're even fiercer than these Silures. Barbarians, all.' He muttered, 'That would be my worst – er –'

'Nightmare?' suggested David.

Edryn clenched his fists and began to move forward.

'Ah!' David grasped his friend's shoulder and pulled him back. 'We hear it's a lot colder up there, don't we, brother? Wetter, too.' He sighed. 'Ice and snow in the long winters.' He looked sad. 'Of course, the emperor can send you anywhere. Our father told us tales of the tribes in the east. Strangely shaped heads.' David shrugged. 'Much better to return to Sicily – or Rome. Or stay here. Then again there's Burr – Burrium.'

Tarquin glared at him. 'This port, Isca, will soon be far more important than Burrium.'

Ah, I think I've needled him. Was it the same the last time we met, I wonder? I can't help myself... I should remember all those courses with the Goddess. What did she say? When you are with someone who believes they are totally right, smile, agree, and walk away. No point in arguing. The trouble is, I can't walk away, not yet...

The young soldier sniggered. 'You must be disappointed to hear that news. But then, here at Isca, the tides are higher, so bigger ships can unload their cargo here. The grain, wine and oil can be sent up north, to Deva Victrix and on to Eboracum.'

He laughed. 'Ah! That's why your father has sent you here, to set up the new routes for trading!' Wagging his finger at them, he said, 'It wasn't just to take back some oil to Burrium. I knew that was just a story. But,' he tapped his nose, 'you can tell me.'

'You've guessed!' David smiled. *We need to get away from him – fast!*

'Could we bathe first? We're very dirty and we – er – Romans like to bath, scrape the dirt off. If you point us in the direction of the Baths – the public ones?'

'I'm a leader here. I can give you permission to use the Legion's Baths.'

Tarquin shouted over to the soldiers, 'March to the amphitheatre. Practice drills until I come!' Turning to the two boys he said, 'Follow me.'

Chapter 6

At Isca

Simone stood on the riverbank, staring into the waters as they swirled past. She didn't notice a salmon leap, or a water vole nibbling at some grasses.

We're here to search for a talisman. But what is it? The Riddle said, "Find something rare". To the tribe, everything Roman is rare. To me, it's like being at home; the Colosseum, the Arch of Titus, temples... Old ruins. She sighed. *I should've taken the Bronze Mirror. I'd have been somewhere else by now – but where? Back to Rome? To my parents?* She gulped. *But they don't want me. Their lives are so busy, they've no time for me....*

'It's all a big mess,' she cried as she juggled the nail back and forth. The sharp end dug into her palm. 'Ouch!'

She looked over to the woods. 'I don't feel a part of the team. Tara and Mariad have made friends – but who's my friend? I haven't got one.' Tears began to trickle down her cheeks. 'What did the Seer say? "Remember the words." Spells, chants... Well, she didn't see this coming! Scary old witch!' she cried. 'I'll show her!'

And with that, Simone threw the nail with all her force towards the river.

'Protect the – the Romans!' she shouted up to the sky.

The nail flew up, curved, and dropped down into the muddied bank.

Turning towards the fortress, she saw two soldiers marching towards her. *Oh no! Are they going to throw me in the dungeons? Help me, someone!*

The legionaries were coming closer. Simone was terrified. *Don't look at them. Be Cleopatra. Stand tall. Be confident.*

Straightening her back, she fixed her eyes on a heron that was standing like a statue on the opposite bank.

The soldiers halted in front of her and saluted.

'The governor, Sextus Julius Frontius, requests that the Priestess Livia come to his residence.'

'However, the priestess is not at the Temple of Diana.'

'As you are her assistant, we will escort you to headquarters.'

Assistant Priestess? Simone glanced down at her clothes. A rough cloth tunic. 'First, I must go to the temple. Escort me there. Now.'

Glide, glide; that's what a priestess would do.

Arriving in front of the temple, the soldiers stopped.

Simone gazed up at the building, with its wide marble steps. *It's like the temples in Rome. There'll be a kind of hall, an atrium, with some chambers off it. Kitchens are at the back, but this is the only entrance and exit. I can't just run out the back and escape.*

As she walked up the steps, her thoughts tumbled over each other. *I must find a robe, some sort of long, flowing dress. And a veil – something to cover my hair. Do I have to braid it?*

In the atrium, she noticed the sacred flame was low and flickering.

It has to be kept alight. Otherwise, there's a harsh punishment. I need to find some twigs... Have I got time? Where's the real priestess?

David and Edryn followed Tarquin through the West Gate, past slaves carrying amphorae full of wine, past rows of hot food stalls. Smells of roasted pork, fish and duck wafted through the air.

'You haven't got these stalls in Burrium,' boasted Tarquin. 'I know.'

David peered at the dishes, sniffing each one as they walked along.

'All this looks terrific!' he whispered to his friend. 'It's been hours since breakfast.'

But Edryn was admiring the paintings of animals underneath the counters: a barking dog; a cockerel crowing; fish swimming in a blue pool.

'Look! Aren't they beautiful?'

Tarquin turned left, past a courtyard, and stopped by a large open pool.

The young Silures stood still, staring in astonishment.

'This pool has just been finished. The Baths are behind. Follow me,' said the soldier. As they walked on, Edryn gasped; in front of them was a massive timber building.

'What is it? It's huge,' he whispered to David.

'This – this is the exercise hall.' Tarquin waved his hand around. 'Of course, it's far superior to the ones you have in Burrium.' He smirked. 'And this swimming pool is the biggest and best in Britannia. Look at the fountain house!'

Edryn could not take his eyes off it. There were paintings of garden scenes, cherubs, gods and goddesses, and a large carved stone dolphin. Water was gushing from its mouth and cascading down marble steps. Behind was a statue of a woman.

'That must be one of their goddesses,' whispered

Edryn. 'Their craftsmen have great gifts.'

'The Greeks taught them...' began David, then said loudly, 'This is magnificent. Very like Pompeii.'

Tarquin raised an eyebrow. 'You've been to Pompeii?'

David nodded. *It isn't a lie, exactly. Last month, I watched an awesome TV documentary about it.*

'This must be better.' Tarquin pulled his shoulders back and puffed out his chest. 'Everything here is better. Our governor, Sextus Julius Frontius, is a genius – the best engineer in the Empire.'

David groaned inwardly. *Everything is bigger and better than anywhere else. He must be very insecure to be like this. A boaster. He reminds me of someone. Stick-out ears. Who is he?*

'Come. I'll show you the changing room, then the plunge bath; after that, the cold, warm and hot rooms.'

Glancing around at the empty Baths, the soldier said, 'I must go and drill my men. Make sure they are perfect for the Games.' He half turned away. 'Everyone is preparing for tomorrow. You'll have the place to yourselves. I'll come back later.'

Tarquin strode off.

'Cool. Now we can have a good squint around,' said David.

'Shouldn't we get back to the woods? Meet up with the girls?'

'We won't be long. And we can report all this back

to the tribe. Tell them what's happening here.'

In the first room, on either side, was a line of seats and a drain that ran down the middle.

'What's this place for?'

'Latrines.' David wrinkled his nose. 'Ergh – severely stinky. Let's move on.'

Edryn pointed to a sponge. 'Those things on sticks – what do they do with them?'

'They clean themselves after going to the loo, the toilet... They're sponges. We use soft paper. You use leaves.'

'Ergh – disgusting!' Edryn grimaced. 'But we can't stay. We have to hear the second riddle, and search for the talisman.'

David patted his friend on the shoulder. 'And we will. Chill! A few minutes here in the Baths won't make any difference. Let's dive in this pool! I didn't have a shower this morning. Or yesterday, come to think of it, at Nanny Lita's!'

'But—'

'It'll be fine. You heard him. Everyone's busy preparing for the games. Let's jump in.'

'But – the talisman – the riddle...'

David was staring down into the pool.

'Look – can you see those sparkling things on the bottom? I'll just dive – Oh! Argh! This is the severely freezing pool!'

As the girls arrived back from burying the third nail, a fox padded along the track behind them and vanished into the undergrowth.

'No one's here except us,' said Mariad. 'Where are they?'

Tara scanned the meadow, the riverbank, and then the fortress. A movement by the South Gate caught her eye.

Taking hold of her friend's arm, she said, 'Look! That's Simone. She's wearing a long dress and a veil over her head.'

'Has she been arrested?'

'I'll climb up for a better look.'

Tara clambered up some low branches. 'I can just see her. She's walking between two soldiers – they're at the entrance. Now they're waiting at the gate.'

Mariad called up, 'Are you sure that's Simone?'

'I'd know her walk anywhere.'

'What do you think has happened?' cried Mariad.

'Maybe they found her when she was burying the nail,' said Tara.

'But,' said Mariad, 'she was going to the East Gate. Why is she there? And she's dressed—'

'Like a Roman priestess,' said Tara. *Oh Simone. What have you done? You've ruined our plan. This is a disaster!*

She sent a mind-message to David. *Simone's been arrested – she'll be thrown in the dungeons.*

Nothing.

Speak to me, Twin!

No reply.

'I've sent a message to David, but it's not getting through.'

'Mars, their god, he must be stopping it,' said Mariad.

A raven cawed, clattered, and whirled up into the sky.

Clutching her bag, Tara ran her fingers over the Bronze Mirror. *Help, Goddess – tell us, what can we do?*

The two girls looked at each other.

'We'll have to search for the talisman on our own,' said Mariad.

'But first – we have to get inside the fortress and rescue Simone,' said Tara.

Her friend shrugged her shoulders.

'We can't abandon her, Mariad. Afterwards, we can search for the talisman.'

'Look at us,' said Mariad. 'We're girls. The fortress is full of men, of soldiers. Only a few families live outside the fortress. You and I would be noticed immediately.'

'I know! A disguise!' said Tara. 'We can put caps over our hair.'

'Will that work?'

'It might. We've done it before,' said Tara. 'Did

you say there were workshops by the wharf?'

'Yes – stonemasons, butchers, blacksmith, leather—'

'A leather shop? There's bound to be caps there! Let's go!'

With great elegance, Simone walked between the two soldiers along the track and towards the South Gate.

I'm terrified. But I mustn't look afraid. I am Cleopatra. Look straight ahead. Do not look at these guards....

They arrived at the entrance.

'Password?'

'Remus.'

'It's quiet around here. Where's the rest of the legion?' asked the taller soldier.

The sentry yawned. 'Over in the amphitheatre practising combat skills, drills – the usual...'

'All day?'

'You know Linus Paulinus. Everything has to be perfect for our centurion.'

The guards glanced at Simone and waved them through the gate to the main street.

She walked along the via principalis as if in a dream.

At the entrance to a courtyard, the soldiers halted.

'Enter, Priestess.'

She walked forward and blinked. She was in a garden.

What a beautiful place!

Four large terracotta pots stood in each corner. In the centre was a sundial. Shrubs of lavender and rosemary were on either side of the paths. Over by some long windows was a marble seat. A pair of goldfinches were sipping from a fountain.

O bellissimo! And the smell from those bushes is—

'This way, Priestess.'

What's going to happen to me now?

She entered a light, airy room.

This must be where the governor lives. My heart – Oh, it's beating so fast. Will he find out I'm not a priestess and arrest me? This is scary. Why didn't I just bury that rusty old nail?

'The governor requests that you wait here in the atrium. He has some business to attend to first.'

The soldiers bowed and left.

They believe I'm a real priestess, thought Simone. *Maybe I won't be arrested.* Glancing around, she noticed a couch in front of a wooden screen. On a table nearby were bowls full of dates, grapes, and pistachios. She perched on the edge of the couch, then leant back. *On one elbow – that's how the Roman emperors did it...*

She chose some grapes.

Oh! Sweet! Much nicer than that awful food up in the hillfort. I think I'll just nibble on some of these pistachios.

She adjusted her veil and gazed around. The walls were covered with paintings.

That looks like a scene of the countryside around Rome.

She turned around and gaped at the painting behind her. *Is that a god?*

Snakes had wrapped themselves around a child. He was fighting them off.

Perhaps that's Hercules as a baby.

She looked up at the ceiling. It was covered in delicate blue flowers, and gold leaves.

This is my kind of place: amazing paintings; lovely food; a fountain. Not muddy floors with chickens running around, an old stinky animal blanket thing to sleep under, and nasty nettle soup to eat. Ergh!

Picking up a bowl, she ran her fingers over the decoration.

'Samian-ware; so beautiful,' she murmured.

Across the room, on a plinth, was the head of a man. *Curly hair, a laurel wreath. It must be an emperor. Julius Caesar? Claudius?*

She shrugged. *They all look the same.*

As she was trying to remember the names of all the emperors, a deep voice came from behind the screen. She froze.

'Is the writing tablet ready?'

'Yes, sir.'

'Let's begin. *Salve.* Greetings to you.'

Simone sat up straight. *The governor – He must be dictating a letter. This could be useful. But who for? The Silures?* She felt torn. *I need to listen to this.*

'No, I'll write to my family first, Philippus. Then the Emperor.'

'Sir.'

'I hope that in this month of July you and our daughter are in good health and are now at our villa at Tivoli. Rome will be far too hot for you during these summer months.'

That's true, thought Simone. *Maybe that's why my parents sent me here?*

'Here at Isca, I continue to work for the glory of Rome and our dear Emperor Vespasian –' *Vespasian? I don't remember him. Was he one of the mad ones?* – 'establishing Roman law here in Britannia, the most western part of our Empire.' He paused.

'Tomorrow, we honour our divine God, Apollo. Three days of Games are to be held in the new amphitheatre. Our soldiers will enjoy this spectacle. As you know, I dislike these events, but the Legion has worked hard. They deserve some entertainment. Bears, wolves, and wild boar will be hunted in the arena. More gladiators will arrive soon from Egypt – three men, two women...'

Women gladiators? I didn't know that...

'The port is finished. There are new wharfs and a customs house with a courtyard, so all is ready for the grain we are expecting. More barracks have been built for the cohorts arriving from Gaul; they will be eager to fight. Archers from Syria, too – they will be going on to the north...'

Simone caught her breath. *More soldiers! This is terrible news for the Silures. But, why should I care?*

But she did. As she slid up the couch nearer to the room, she heard: 'Linus Paulinus remains the senior centurion here. You will remember he fought with Titus, son of our emperor, in Judea, and crushed the Hebrews. Afterwards, he served with General Suetonius here in Britannia. Oh, how he hated the Druids and all the tribes! His greatest wish was to destroy them all.'

Simone heard footsteps pacing up and down the chamber. A pause.

'The tribe here, the Silures, are fierce, stubborn people. They could attack us at any time. The centurion asks when I will give the order for the battle.'

A heavy sigh. 'I hope that they will not provoke us. If they do, I'll have no choice but to—'

The footsteps stopped.

Is he coming to see me now?

'Oh – rub all that out. My wife and daughter don't want to hear about war and battles.'

The voice came nearer. Simone heard him murmur.

'But why – why can't the tribe accept *Pax Romana*, the Peace of Rome? The tribes in the south of Britannia have. They pay taxes to us; they learn our language, our customs. We let them worship their own gods...'

Simone leaned nearer, trying to catch his next words.

'No, don't write that, either. I'm thinking aloud. Begin again...'

He cleared his throat. 'At the shrine here to Apollo, I pray daily for your health and happiness and that of our daughter, Divinia. I pray too that the Silures will accept our laws, our rule, and there will be peace soon.' A pause. A whisper. 'To resist the might and power of our Empire is to choose death. I've had enough of death.'

The footsteps became more hurried.

'How is our dear daughter? She will be 14 next year. Soon, she must be married. We must decide on a suitable husband.'

*She's 14? I'll be 14 in two years' time. Married? And her parents are arranging it? She can't choose – she can't even choose **not** to get married. What a nightmare! My parents wouldn't do that to me.*

The governor's voice came closer.

'You will be happy to know that I am designing the gardens and the mosaics for our new villa in Herculaneum. I've decided on spirals, circles, squares, all in interesting patterns. I trust you will like them.'

He cleared his throat.

'Now that Julius Agricola, the new governor, has arrived in Britannia, I hope to be leaving for Rome before the winter storms come. Know that I am, as always, your loving husband, Sextus Julius Frontius.'

There was another deep sigh.

'And may peace be made with the tribe before I leave...'

Simone sat up straight.

'Give me my seal. Send this letter on the next ship.'

So the governor wants peace but this centurion wants to attack the Silures. The children – the people – they could all be killed. Killed.

She groaned. *I didn't bury the nail. I didn't say the spell. It'll be my fault if the Silures are attacked and die...* She wanted to cry. *I've made a terrible mistake. But it's too late now. Too late.*

As she closed her eyes, an image flashed into her mind, of the little girl in the tomb begging for help. She bit her lip.

'Priestess?'

A tall man with piercing blue eyes stood in front of her.

Grey hair; a long, narrow nose – he could be a Roman emperor! He swept his toga over his shoulder.

'Ah, I was expecting the priestess Livia.' He smiled. 'Now I remember. She's gone to Burrium – or perhaps Blestium – for a few days. You must be her assistant.'

Simone nodded and stared at the mosaic floor; patterns, colours of red, blue, green, gold-yellow.

'So.' He placed his hand on his heart and bowed. 'Assistant Priestess of the Goddess Diana. Forgive me for keeping you waiting. Please come in. We have to discuss the Games.'

Up in the hillfort, the Seer was sitting under the rowan tree. In her hands was an object; long, purple, pointed. She bent over it, whispering, chanting. Then, taking a leather pouch, she placed the object inside and drew the strings tightly.

Over at the forge, Aled was working. Another blade. Another weapon. Sparks flew. Chickens scattered. He stopped to wipe the sweat from his face. Glancing around the clearing, he noticed Bryn slipping away into the woods. The blacksmith frowned.

Bethan looked up from her bone. *That man – is he going to see my friend?*

Perhaps I can go with him....

She began to stretch her back legs.

The Seer threw her a stern look.
And then again... Maybe not...

From the slope above the quay, Tara and Mariad scanned the scene below them. The screams and cries of children diving in and out of the workshops drifted up to them. A butcher was chopping up the carcass of a deer. Further along, a stone mason was working, chiselling an inscription onto a huge piece of stone.

At the wharf, a merchant was shouting orders to a group of slaves.

'Take those sacks of grain to the Customs House. Carry them through the courtyard!'

Mariad sighed. 'See how they've settled here. Unless the gods and goddesses give us a miracle, they'll stay. Their ships arrive here loaded with grain. They store some of it there, in those new buildings. That goes to their fortresses in the north. See the biggest building? The Custom House? They use it to control what comes in and goes out of the port.'

As she looked around, Tara caught a glimpse of a short, swarthy figure; the person looked left and right, and then crept behind the Customs House. *That looks like Bryn. Can it be? What's he doing here?*

Mariad gripped her friend's arm. 'If we make for the back of the workshops, we might find two caps there. And find out what's happening.'

The two girls scrambled down the slope and hid behind the leather shop.

Voices drifted across from the riverside.

'We need to complete this work before sunset,' bellowed a square-shouldered soldier. 'We're expecting more ships – bigger ships – in the next few days. And the games begin tomorrow. This new wharf must be finished today.'

He paced up and down. 'Perhaps you'd like to fight in the arena instead; face starving bears, wolves, and wild boar – famished, all of them! Ready for flesh – any kind of flesh.' He paused. 'Now get on with it!'

Chapter 7

At the Baths

David heaved himself out of the pool and placed some gemstones on the ledge.

Then he noticed a glass vessel.

'I wonder what this is. Do you know, Edryn?'

His friend shook his head; he was still staring around at the Baths in amazement.

'It looks like a flask. I wonder what's in it. Water? Oil?'

Taking off the top, David sniffed it.

'Wow! Awesome! It smells like rosemary. Or lavender?' He began smearing the liquid all over his arms.

'Oh, I smell great!' said David. 'Try some. Simone would be furious if she knew we were here. She's probably crawling around in some muddy ditch!'

'Beautiful!' Edryn was looking at the gems. 'This one's purple! And it's carved; a woman with a flower. And, by all the Heavens! Here's a mouse eating a twig! Why have they left them in the pool?'

'Maybe they've dropped out of rings?'

David dived in again and brought up a long, thin metal object. At the end of it was a tiny cup filled with yellow stuff.

He poked it. 'What's this inside the cup?' He grimaced. 'Ergh! Severely yukky! Ear wax!'

After diving again, he found a small, cream-coloured knife, and a long, curved piece of silver. He laid them down by his friend.

'What do they do with that metal thing?' asked Edryn.

'I think it's a kind of scraper. For getting off dirt? Give it a go.'

'An important person must own this.' Edryn stared closely at it. 'It's made of silver and gold; there are pictures on it... twelve different pictures of a man... A god? Could it belong to the governor?'

'Maybe.'

As the young boy began scraping mud off his elbows, he said, 'Caratacus might be bathing in a place like this now.'

David was peering at the mosaic at the bottom of the pool; three dolphins leaping in a blue sea.

'Did you say he was a prisoner?'

'No, he was freed, pardoned by the Emperor,

Claudius. Ah. A brave leader he was. What a warrior!'

David raised his hand to stop Edryn. 'Wait. I have to listen to my sister...'

Where are you, Twin? I've been sending mind-messages to you.

David looked confused. *Tara. I haven't got them. Something must've been blocking them. That's weird.*

It is. It's never happened before. Mariad thinks it could be their war god. Mars.

Maybe. So, what's up? Did you bury the nail?

We did. But Simone's been arrested. She's been taken inside the fortress. We have to rescue her, then find the talisman. We need you both, and quickly. Meet us by the edge of the woods...

David looked around for a towel to dry his hair. *Alright. First, I just have to – er – do something.*

Twin – Are you in some kind of water?

Er – won't be long, Tara. We're coming now...

Putting the flask down, David said, 'Oh wild! Let's go this second! Tara and Mariad are waiting for us. And Simone's been arrested.'

'What? How do you know?'

'My twin's sent me a message – she whizzes it into my mind.' He frowned. 'Oh, I'm in the most massive trouble. Don't mention the Baths.'

Edryn threw down the silver scraper and leapt up.

'What were we thinking of? My father will be so angry with me. And Bryn – furious, he'll be. All the tribe, too. We've been sent to find this rare thing, and here we are – playing.'

As they were pulling on their tunics, the boys heard a voice behind them. 'So – you're spies.'

David groaned. *Edryn was right.* He swivelled around, smiling.

'Spies? Us? No! We told you. Father wants to send goods to the north; grain, oil, fish sauce, pistachios...'

Tarquin glared at him. 'You spoke of Caratacus. A brave leader, you said. A warrior. The one who was captured, sent to Rome, a prisoner, and in chains. He is your hero.'

I'll stare straight into his eyes – that'll convince him, thought David.

'We were just saying that Father saw him there; that the great emperor Claudius spared his life – pardoned him – er—'

Please help me, Goddess. I've messed up – again...

'Ed – Edrynus ... Eddidus – my brother here – he mentioned Caratacus's name – nothing more.'

Edryn fixed his gaze on the dolphins. *Please, one of you – open your huge mouth now, and swallow me. Let me swim with you, away, away to the source of the river. And take my friend David, too.*

'You said "our" leader.'

'Er – no – I don't think so—'

'Are you saying I'm deaf?' Tarquin moved towards David, his hand on his scabbard. David tried not to gulp. Instead, he coughed. 'Perhaps with all the water cascading down the steps of that magnificent fountain over there, or the pipes gurgling with the hot water... What a great invention, by the way... this under-floor heating.' David waved his hand vaguely in the direction of the hypocaust. 'Can't beat it. It's catching on. We're having it put in next week—'

Leaning towards Tarquin, he whispered, 'My brother does mumble at times.'

The young soldier glowered at him. 'You have answers for everything.'

He took a step back. 'You two have come here to find something rare. And don't tell me I didn't hear that.'

'Rare?' David thought quickly. 'Yes! Almonds from Siberinnia. They are so rare. Father wants to find those especially. Very expensive, they are.' David cast around for answers. *What rhymes with rare?*

'And... we're expecting to see a bear in his lair. Lair... rare... bear...' David smiled.

Sorry bears, you know I believe no one should ever harm you. It's just we are in a tight spot here. It's terrible they make you fight in their amphitheatres. Barbarians.

Tarquin walked around the two boys. He thrust his head towards David; his nose inches away.

That nose – I know it! I know him!

'You've a secret. Open your right hand. Show me what's there!'

'My hand? A secret?'

'You're holding something—'

David clenched his fist. 'What? No...'

Grabbing hold of his hand, Tarquin forced his fingers open.

'Gemstones! Thieves! You came here to steal.'

David shook his head. 'No – I'm interested in different gems. I found these when I dived into this swimming pool – which is splendid, by the way – what a great pool. Olympic standard. These were lying on the bottom. Look.' He pointed to each one. 'Aren't they beautiful? Take them. Give them back to the owners. I don't want to keep them. I just like looking at them. See – this is an agate, and here's amber – amethyst and rose quartz, too... The carvings on them, they're totally brilliant...'

Tarqin raged at him. 'Liars! Common thieves! And here's more proof.' Tarquin picked up the long metal object. 'My ear-scraper.'

David shuddered. *Ugh! That's **his** ear wax! I touched it. Oh, mega yuck!*

Tarquin grabbed the knife Edryn was holding.

'And you've got my knife! You are runaway slaves!'

Taking his sword out of his scabbard, he pointed it first at David's chest, then at Edryn's.

'I'm taking you to the senior centurion of the Second Augustan Legion. We'll see what he does with you. Throw you to the bears, I expect. Or the gladiators can beat you to death!' He threw his head back and laughed. 'That, I'll enjoy watching!' He went behind the boys and jabbed David in the back. 'Now move!'

David stumbled forward. *Oh, this is not good.*

'Go on!' Tarquin pushed Edryn forwards.

Outside, the boys blinked and covered their eyes. In front of them was a broad-shouldered figure, a crest on his helmet, and armour glinting in the midday sun. He was carrying a cudgel in his left hand, and a spear in his right.

'Gaius Tarquin Livinius! What is the meaning of this?' he barked, holding up the spear.

'This *pilum* was lying around the Exercise Hall. Are you responsible?'

The young soldier stood to attention and saluted. 'Sir. I believe that one belongs to Flavius—'

'You believe? *You believe?*' shouted the centurion. 'Since he is a hostage, held by those savages up there in the hillfort, that is easy to say. Nothing is ever your fault, is it?'

Tarquin chewed his lip.

'Why is your sword drawn?'

'I – er—' Tarquin took a breath. 'Sir... you see—'

'Who are these boys?'

Puffing himself up, the soldier announced, 'Spies. Traitors. Thieves. Runaway slaves. Sir.'

Linus Paulinus frowned. 'They can't be all four. Choose one.'

'I found them outside our defences, sir. By the

West Gate. This one...' He waved his sword at David. 'He told me that they'd come from Burrium; that his father had been a governor of Cas – Sal – li... er... Anyway – a province in the east, and that now he's a merchant.' He moved to stand next to the centurion.

'Continue.'

'Yes, sir. He said their father sent them here to check on pottery – amphorae – or oil, or something...'

'Or something ...?' The centurion looked the boys up and down. 'And they were in the new Baths built for the Legion because?'

Tarquin coughed. 'He said he'd been to Pompeii. Er – and his father saw – er – Caratacus in Rome – leader of the—'

'Silence! I know who Caratacus is!' The centurion narrowed his eyes. 'Tell me, when that barbarian was brought in chains to Rome, to our Emperor Claudius, what was given to each Roman citizen?'

I need to give an answer, any answer.

'A bag of silver *denarii*.'

'Each?' Linus Paulinus raised an eyebrow. 'So much?'

Ah, perhaps that wasn't – quick... I need to say something...

'The Emperor Claudius was most generous,' said David.

'Your father was a slave there.'

David breathed deeply. 'No – he was governor of

a province in the east of the Empire.' He smiled. 'That was before I was born, of course.'

'Of course.'

Scowling, the centurion walked in a circle around the boys. He poked David in the chest with the spear.

'You – you're a liar and, I believe – a slave. A runaway slave. You know what we do to them?'

Horror pictures raced through David's mind. *Spartacus, Christians thrown to lions in the Colosseum, and finishing with...* He gulped.

The centurion turned to Tarquin. 'Tell them. Those who are cowards or traitors we—'

'Stone them to death.' The young soldier grinned.

'Those who rebel against us, like the slave leader, Spartacus, we—'

'Nail them to a cross.' Tarquin smiled broadly.

'But, I've a better idea,' said the centurion. 'Tomorrow is the Festival of Apollo. We need something different – something interesting for the men. Fresh entertainment.' He nodded. 'Yes, you can pit your strength in the arena against the wild beasts. Or – if you survive – the gladiators.'

'Or all of them,' added Tarquin, grinning.

'We'll enjoy watching the spectacle.' Linus Paulinus glanced at Edryn. 'You, little boy, you'll not last long.'

Trying not to shake with fear, the young Silures clenched his fists.

Tarquin spoke again, hoping to get on the

centurion's good side. 'I overheard them say they were looking for something inside the fortress, sir. Something rare.'

'In actual fact...' began David.

The centurion sneered. 'Anything to slaves is rare. They have nothing. Like those savages up the hill.'

Edryn rushed forward, holding up his fists, ready to punch him. 'Fight you to our last breath, we will,' he shouted. 'Our land – you have stolen. Our children – you have killed.'

As David grabbed his friend's arm to pull him back, he noticed a flicker of fear in Tarquin's eyes. *What's he afraid of? There's something...*

'Ah – a Silures.' The centurion narrowed his eyes. 'So fierce for such a young – and very small – boy. All you have to do is to submit to us. Keep our laws. Pay our taxes. We rule you now. This land is ours. We came to bring *Pax Romana.* The Peace of Rome.'

'It's **your** peace,' shouted Edryn. 'Not ours. It's our land. Not yours!'

This gets worse, thought David. *How can we escape?*

Tarquin tugged at his ear and gloated. 'Britannia is now part of the glorious Roman Empire.'

Yes, it is him. Those stick-out ears. Those eyes. He tried to steal the treasure from us in the first task. When we met him first, in Monmouth Castle, he was Tristran. One and the same. Here he's Tarquin. My arch enemy is here again, goading me, pushing me to the edge of anger.

Came a whisper:

A lesson for you, time traveller. Learn to be silent.

He ignored the warning and blurted out, 'Years from now, Britannia won't belong to you. It won't **be** a Roman colony. You'll leave this island and return to Rome. Why? Because your city will be burning. Your enemies will overrun you and destroy your empire. No more Roman Empire!'

He waved his hand to include the fortress. 'This place will be a ruin. People will come to visit it in two thousand years' time and take photos – er – paint pictures – and stare at the old bits of mosaics in your Baths.'

There was a long silence.

Came a whisper:

You should not have spoken of this...

He shivered.

The centurion frowned. 'A slave and a Silures. Rebels. Trouble-makers. And a would-be prophet, too!'

He turned to Tarquin. 'March them to the amphitheatre. Throw them in the dungeons under the arena. Tomorrow, they will face Nemesis. To live. To die. That's where their Fate will be decided.

The governor was standing next to Simone in the courtyard, pointing to the fountain. 'This water comes from pipes that I—'

A soldier stood in the entrance and saluted.

'What is it?' He glanced at the legionary.

'Sir. The centurion has ordered me to go down into the vault. I'm to take the legion's standard to the arena. To practise for the parade, sir.'

Julius Frontius nodded. Turning to Simone, he said, 'May I ask you to accompany us down into the vault? We can pray together at the shrine to Mars.'

Simone froze. *A vault? Small. Creepy. Dark. This is a nightmare. What shall I do? Refuse and be discovered as a fraud? I'd spend the rest of my life in a dungeon. Or do I go down...?*

'Come, Priestess.'

She took some steps forward into the governor's room.

There, he pointed to a screen in the corner.

'Set this aside.'

In the floor was a wooden door with an iron ring. *Oh no! A trap door. Is this the dungeon?*

The soldier grasped hold of the ring and lifted the door up. A flight of stairs led down into darkness.

O Dio mio! It's as black as night in there. Panic caught her throat.

'Light the passage.'

'Sir.' The soldier clattered down the narrow stone steps.

Simone's heart was beating fast. *Is this a trick? Does he know I'm a fraud? Does he know I'm not a priestess? I could be imprisoned here forever. Like the Count of Monte Cristo.*

'All's ready, sir.'

'Go down first. Light our way. I shall descend next; the priestess will follow.' He turned to Simone. 'There are several passages under here. It's a warren! At the bottom of the stairs, we'll turn right and go along a passage. It leads to the shrine room. The strong room is down another passage.'

He smiled. 'The soldiers must be paid today, before the Games start. They'll want to place their bets on their favourite gladiator!'

Simone hesitated. She continued to stare at the open door.

A damp, stuffy, stale smell drifted up. *Will my feet move? Will I be able to breathe down there? I could be buried alive. No one would ever know. My parents...*

'It's safe,' said the governor. 'Come. Torches have been lit all along the passage for us to see our way.'

Hardly listening, she put her foot onto the first step.

At the end of the long passage was a small, square room. Shadows danced over the walls. Flames flickered, picking out shapes; helmets, shields, swords, spears. Then, as Simone's eyes became used to the gloom, she saw a figure standing on a stone bench. A statue. Mars, God of War!

From head to foot, the girl trembled. *What am I doing here? Why has he brought me to this horrible place? Shall I confess everything? That I'm not a priestess? That I'm a fraud? Will I tell him about the nails? That we are looking for a talisman? Will he show me mercy? The Romans never show mercy. O Goddess, Aiuto! Help! Save me!*

The governor was speaking to the soldier. 'Wait here. When we leave, take the standard to the arena. Then tell the clerk to come here and go to the strong room. He must make an exact record for the soldiers' pay.'

'Sir.'

'Now, we will pray to Mars...'

Twisting a gold signet ring on his little finger, the governor stood in front of the shrine.

Seconds passed. A minute.

Turning towards Simone, he said, 'Did the Priestess make a votive offering to the Goddess Diana before she left for Burrium? Asking for protection for us – for the Second Augustan Legion?'

Simone crossed her fingers behind her back and nodded.

'Did she have a message for me?'

Oh! What would a priestess say?

He prompted. 'A message from the Goddess Diana?'

Remembering a Latin proverb from school, she whispered, '*Festina lente.*'

'*Festina lente.* Good. Yes. Make haste slowly.

Don't rush into anything... Our great emperor Augustus said that often. A wonderful saying!'

He gazed at the statue of Mars. 'Did she say anything else?'

Simone could not move, could not speak.

'Ah, no. No.'

What's he thinking? Perhaps he's disappointed with the message. When in doubt, be silent. Tara says that.

He took a step towards the shrine. Simone felt the eyes of the god fixed upon her; cruel, glowering, vengeful.

'Let us offer prayers for a successful Games tomorrow.'

Pretend to pray. But not to Mars, God of War! Never! I am praying, though – to someone. Anyone – the Goddess! Please get me out of here!

She looked at the array of weapons and shuddered.

After several minutes of silence, the Governor turned towards her. 'Priestess. Will you grace us with your presence at the opening of the Games tomorrow, to honour Apollo? And preside over the rituals?'

Rituals? I don't know any rituals. How will I know what to do? When is the real priestess coming back? If she finds me here, I'll be toast, as David says. Oh, I want to be with my cousins. When will this nightmare end? I have to agree.

She bowed.

'Excellent. I thank you.' *She looks so like my dear daughter, Divinia.*

Sighing, he turned to the soldier. 'Now, you may take the standard...'

At the top of the stairs, he called, 'Guards. Escort the priestess back to the Temple of Diana. Tell the centurion I wish to see him urgently.'

Dazed, Simone walked through the streets back to the Temple.

At the Games tomorrow, I have to act like a priestess. If I get the rituals wrong, they'll punish me, maybe kill me. Wall me up. They used to do that...

She choked back tears as she remembered her words to David in the graveyard.

"I don't need protecting." *But I do. Who will help me escape from this – this horror?*

Chapter 8

The Second Riddle

The girls were crouching down at the back of the workshops when Mariad noticed a tall solder, a crest on his helmet, striding along the riverbank towards the quay.

He stopped. Then, casting his eyes over the new buildings, he walked under the main archway and into the courtyard.

'That's Linus Paulinus, the centurion. He likes to know everyone's business,' said Mariad as she tugged at her friend's arm. 'Let's creep in closer and listen to this...'

'*Ah, Centurion! Salve!*

A grunt.

'Have you heard any news about my ships?' asked a merchant. 'They should've arrived by now.'

'Ah, Tiberius Blandus and Ventus Maximus, you're here, too. No. No news.'

Linus Paulinus waved towards the river. 'Tides, winds...'

The girls peered around an open door. There was the centurion, hand resting on his scabbard, staring at the piles of sacks.

'My ships are bringing the finest oil and grain, too,' said the plump man, clasping his hands together. 'Unless they arrive soon, I shall be ruined! Ruined!'

'We're expecting figs and a variety of nuts as well,' said his friend.

The centurion noticed a wasp landing on his cloak. He squashed it and smiled.

'Cohorts, that's the most important thing they're carrying. More soldiers to fight and destroy these tribes once and for all.'

'Er – I see. Certainly, our local tribe here is quite stubborn – one might even say – er – fierce,' said Blandus.

'Fierce? We're all fierce!' the centurion shouted. 'But we don't skulk in woods, rush out, attack the enemy, and vanish into the trees. No! We are disciplined – and we will crush them. Crush them! Do you hear me, Tiberius Blandus?'

'Oh, I do. I do.' The merchant rubbed the side of his nose. 'And I'm sure you will, Linus Paulinus. Crush them. You're the man to do it. You and your fine legion here. After all, you were in Judea with

Titus, the emperor's son.'

I wonder what's annoyed him today, thought the merchant. *He is in a temper.*

Glancing over his shoulder, the centurion lowered his voice.

'The thing is – the governor doesn't want to fight.'

Although they'd heard the rumours, both merchants looked shocked.

'Not fight?' said Blandus. 'But Sextus Julius Frontius fought in Gaul; he destroyed the tribes there.'

'Like Caesar before him,' added Ventus.

'And brutally, too. Or so I've heard.'

'True. Now he prefers to give instructions about laying pipes and shoring up the riverbank. Plans for new drains – they take up all his time.' The centurion heaved a heavy sigh. 'Still, he'll be returning to Rome within a few weeks – to build his new villa in Herculaneum.'

'Oh, very nice.'

The centurion scowled. 'It's fortunate that our new governor has arrived in Britannia. Now Julius Agricola – he intends to fight.'

Standing with legs apart, hands on his hips, he spat. 'Drains! Pipes! I, Linus Paulinus, am a soldier of the Second Augustan Legion. I came here to engage with the enemy, not drain fields.'

The merchants exchanged looks.

'And what of the games?' asked Blandus. 'Will you take some time for enjoyment? For entertainment?'

'Tomorrow I will. I've just arrested two boys. They've been thrown into the dungeons. A night listening to the wild beasts howling will...'

His words were carried away by the wind as the three men strolled out of the courtyard and walked further along the quayside.

'That's what Flavius, one of the hostages, told Simone,' said Tara. 'This governor likes to build things – barracks; roads. He isn't interested in fighting more battles.'

Mariad frowned. 'Unless something happens, and he won't have a choice.'

'What do you mean?'

'Grain. Some of the warriors want to burn the Custom House down.'

Tara whispered, 'Then there would be bloodshed.'

Clasping the bag to her heart, she felt for the Bronze Mirror inside; it was there, safe. *The only way to stop this battle is to find the talisman.*

'Have you sent another mind-message to your twin?'

'Yes. But – he hasn't answered. The boys could be anywhere.'

Mariad frowned. 'Do you feel something terrible

has happened to them?'

'Maybe. Or David just isn't listening,' said Tara, sighing. 'That's when things always go wrong.'

'Do you think Simone got to the East Gate, buried the nail and said the words?

Tara stared hard at the ground. 'She did promise.'

'But your cousin was angry. If she hasn't buried it, it means the spell won't work. There's nothing to hold the soldiers inside the fortress. They can march out and attack the tribe at any time.'

Tara hesitated. 'She promised.'

'Perhaps she was arrested before she got to the East Gate.' Mariad put her hand to her mouth. 'Oh! Would she tell the governor about our mission, our task?

'No. Simone wouldn't do that.' *But would she?* wondered Tara.

'First, we have to find some caps,' said Mariad.

The two girls slipped out of the courtyard and crept further along the back of the workshops. A pile of boots and sandals were piled up on a bench outside one, waiting to be repaired.

'This must be it,' said Tara.

'If I look in the workshop for the caps,' said Mariad, 'can you keep a look out?'

Tara stood watching. A figure was creeping around the side of the Custom House. *It is Bryn. What's he doing here? In the middle of the day? I must tell Mariad.*

A few minutes later, her friend appeared, holding two leather caps.

'Here's yours.'

'I've just seen—'

'These are perfect!' With a broad smile, Mariad tucked her flaming red hair underneath the cap. 'Let's go!'

'I need to tell you something...'

'Oh no! Too late!' cried Mariad. 'Quick! Hide!'

The plump merchant was moving in their direction. Two slaves behind him were carrying large wooden boxes.

The girls ducked behind some barrels next to the butcher's shop.

Several large dead rabbits were dangling from hooks. Tara pinched her nose and tried not to breathe. *Ugh! What an awful smell!*

'Be careful! Don't drop that box!' shouted the merchant. 'It's fragile! Fragile! That's Samian-ware in there. Pottery! Beautiful pottery! But what would you know!'

One box started to tip.

'Put it down! Put them all down here! Can I trust any of you to carry these? I think not!'

As he walked around the boxes, he called out to the slaves. 'You! Write this down! Felix owes 105 *denarii.* You! Give this barrel to Grassius. Tell him I hear the Silures make barrels better than he does! A good reason to make peace if ever I heard,' he muttered. 'And you – get your sandals repaired.

I don't want to hear you've tripped, broken your leg and smashed any of these amphorae. That would be a great inconvenience to me!'

The slave began running down the track towards the fortress.

'No! That's for the Legion. Go just here – to Victrix's – his workshop is along there. Hurry!'

He sat down heavily on a barrel, breathless. 'I need a few minutes...'

The girls waited. Would he notice them? How long would he stay there?

With the edge of his toga, Tiberius Blandus wiped his brow, shifted his weight, and disturbed a huge black spider.

It scuttled along the top of the nearest box and crept onto the back of his hand.

'What... Argh!' He jumped up. 'A spider! Poison! Deadly! Is there no peace to be had?'

He brushed it off and waddled as fast as he could towards the Custom House.

'Come on, Tara. Let's scramble up here and make for the woods,' Mariad urged.

Grey clouds covered the midday sun. A raven flew across the field and towards the oaks. The girls shivered.

'We need to hear the second riddle,' said Mariad.

Down the via principalis, out through the South Gate and towards the amphitheatre, the soldiers marched the boys.

David was turning over everything in his mind.

What shall I say to Tara? That Edryn and I were arrested in the Baths? She'll ask why. Because I felt like a dip into the Legion's new swimming pool. And tomorrow we'll be fighting for our lives in the arena.

He looked up; a pair of swifts were whirling above them, catching insects on the soft breeze.

Will I ever see my parents again? Nanny Lita and Grandpa... Bethan...? We've been sent on a quest to save this planet and I've messed up – again. I must find a way for us to escape.

He glanced to his right. A cohort was marching up and down a nearby field.

'They're practising for the Games,' grinned the shorter guard.

'Ah! Tomorrow's a good day to die!'

'It is for them, Cornelius! It is for them!'

'Here we are – the amphitheatre. Go in this entrance alive...'

'And be taken out of the other one dead!' said his friend.

Laughing, they pushed the boys through the entrance.

David looked around the arena. *It's like a football stadium. There's a grandstand, made of timber, with tiers of seating. They'll make us fight the wild animals here – or will it be the gladiators? We'll be the entertainment.* He gulped. *If we survive, I promise I'll never ever blurt out anything... And it's my fault Edryn is here.*

He caught a glimpse of his friend's terrified face as the soldiers prodded them down a flight of earthen steps. At the bottom was a narrow, dimly lit passageway,

David took a breath; the smell almost knocked him out. *Animals, people...* He wanted to be sick. *What a stench! This place reeks of blood... Ugh!*

'Turn right, slaves!'

'Can you hear grunts?' muttered Edryn. 'What kind of animals are down here?'

'You'll find out soon enough,' shouted Cornelius. 'Move!'

Stumbling along, they could see cages on either side. As they passed by, several wolves began howling, on and on. Desperate cries were coming from a young bear as it paced around a tiny space. Sticking its face onto the iron bars, it stared out at the boys. *I'm suffering. Help me.*

'I'm sorry,' whispered David. 'Keeping you in a cage. It's brutal. I'll free you – somehow.'

'Early morning – you boys will be facing these,' said the guard.

'We call it "going on a hunt",' chuckled the other. 'Now get in there.'

Thrusting the boys into a tiny chamber, he locked the metal door.

Crouching in the gloom, they wondered what tomorrow would bring. Life or Death?

The two girls, hair tucked well inside their caps, flung themselves down under the trees.

Two green woodpeckers cried above them.

'Calling for rain,' said Mariad.

One began to drill for insects in a nearby oak.

Tara took the Bronze Mirror out of her bag. *O Goddess. Help us. Please show us where the boys and Simone are.*

As she peered into the Mirror, mists swirled, then parted. There were the two boys, huddled together in a small, night-black space. Edryn was holding his head in his hands. David was staring blankly at the walls.

'Oh! Where are they?' cried Tara.

'A dungeon?' said Mariad.

Again, the mists whirled, then showed Simone dressed in a long robe and a veil.

She looked stricken. A grey-haired man in a toga and a soldier holding a flaming torch were standing with her.

'Why is she with those people?' Mariad was shocked. 'And where is she?'

Tara sighed deeply. 'Now we must rescue them all.'

'And then we must find the talisman.'

'Can we do this?' said Tara. *I'm feeling such pressure...*

Putting her hands on her friend's shoulders, Mariad looked deep into her eyes. 'I am the granddaughter of the Seer. Flowing through my mind is the spirit of the Druids, the dreamers. Flowing through my body is the blood of my tribe, the blood of warriors.' She paused. 'Tara. Guardian of the Bronze Mirror. Time traveller, dreamer, peacemaker... I say together we are strong, we are powerful, brave, courageous. We can rescue all three. And – we can find the talisman.'

The girls clasped hands. 'Warriors, both.'

Tara looked into the Mirror. 'May the second riddle be told to us now.'

Came the whisper:

Seek that which is rare
Made from willow and pear.
A circle, strong, yet light,
Held aloft, foes take fright.
Seek that which is rare,
But beware! Beware!
The talisman will be found –
In a lair. In a lair.

Tara put the Mirror back into her bag. 'What's made of willow and pear?'

'Fences for animals?'

'A circle. Strong, yet light.'

'Made of a tree and a fruit,' said Mariad.

'The branch of the pear tree,' said Tara. 'Woven into a circle.'

'If it's held up high, the enemy will be afraid.'

'How is that possible?'

'A circle of magic?' said Mariad.

'Like the sun or the moon? An orb?'

I wish the others were here to talk about it, thought Tara. *This is a mystery...*

'If it's precious to the Silures, why have the Romans got it?' asked Tara.

Mariad shrugged. 'It could've been taken in a battle.'

'What about the last part of the riddle – it's in a lair?'

'Animals live in lairs.'

'What animals do the Romans keep?' asked Tara.

'Oxen, horses. Sheep and goats, chickens and ducks...'

'But none of those live in lairs.'

Mariad cried out. 'They use animals for fighting; wild boar, wolves and bears. They keep them in cages underneath the amphitheatre. The gladiators, they fight the animals; the wilder the better. All the soldiers love it. They shout. Go out of their minds.'

'So, the talisman could be under the arena.'

Looking over towards the river, the girls saw white-grey clouds were sweeping across the sky. The woodpeckers had whipped up a storm.

'What are we going to do first, Tara? Rescue your cousin? Or the boys?'

'We don't know exactly where they are.'

'Should we search for the talisman, then? In a lair?' asked Mariad.

Heavy drops of rain were beginning to fall. They huddled closer to a hedge for some shelter.

Tara hugged her knees tightly. 'I feel we need to sit here and think for a moment.'

At the steps of the Temple of Diana, the soldiers bowed and left. Simone stood staring up at the columns.

Exactly like Rome...

As she entered the atrium, Simone noticed the sacred fire was low, but still burning.

How did that happen? Has the priestess returned? I'd better look around. Then I need to find the prayers for the rituals.

Entering the furthest room, she stopped still. Before her was a statute of the Goddess Diana. Around her neck was a chain of gold with gemstones of every hue: amber, amethyst, citrine, blue agate, rose.

A rainbow. The Goddess. An image of the iron nail hovering, then dropping, flashed into her mind. She bowed her head, covering her face with the veil.

O Goddess. Forgive me. I was angry...

All was silent.

Came a whisper:

A priestess you are, in this time; in this place...

Startled, the girl looked around. No one was there. Who had spoken?

... and under my protection. Tomorrow, you will carry out the sacred rituals.

But I don't know what to do, Goddess.

Enter the chamber on your right. There you will find the sacred scrolls. On them are written the rituals, the prayers. Learn them perfectly.

Grazie. Thank you. Goddess.

Sighing with relief, Simone went into the room. At the far end was a wooden cabinet. As she took out the first roll, she heard a series of loud coughs coming from outside the temple. Placing the papyrus back in the cabinet, she covered her face with the veil. Tiptoeing through the atrium, she hid behind a column and peered down.

At the bottom of the steps was a young soldier clutching a clay tablet. He was looking furtively around him.

I've seen him somewhere before. But where? Now – I need to stand like a priestess.

'Speak.'

'Oh!' He looked at her in astonishment, then quickly bowed.

'Er – Honourable Priestess. I have come here today to – to beg for help.'

Say nothing.

He stared up at her again and glanced quickly away.

'Er – to plead. To – to ask for the protection of the Goddess Diana.'

Silence.

He shuffled his feet. 'May I ask the Goddess to accept this curse – I've written it all out—'

He began walking up the steps, offering the lead tablet to Simone.

What should I do? I can't receive a curse.

Raising her hand, she said, 'Halt!'

He stopped.

'Read!'

Clearing his throat, he began:

'I, Gaius Tarquin Livinius, discovered two boys, Davidus and Eddidus, stealing gemstones from the Baths – as well as my knife and ear thing. A *striglus,* too.' He looked up. 'I think it belongs to the governor, or a tribune. It is made of gold and silver...'

He spat. 'They are thieves, spies, traitors. As I write this, they are in the dungeons under the arena. Tomorrow they will fight for their lives.'

His voice became harsher. 'They will die or – I must kill them.'

Simone felt herself swaying. *What's he saying?* Touching a column, she steadied herself.

'May my foes be defeated at the Games, O Goddess. If anyone knows anything about them, and the reason for their coming here to Isca, may they have all their intestines torn out and eaten by the wildest of beasts!'

David and Edryn have been arrested... They're in a dungeon.

'May I be given great powers by you, O Goddess of the hunt, to defeat, to slay these worthless enemies.'

Oh No! He's going to kill them. If I accept this tablet from him, some wild animal will come and eat my insides. I feel sick. What shall I say, O Goddess?

Simone fixed her eyes on the hills across the river and took a deep breath. A light breeze brushed her face. When she spoke, her voice was deep, powerful. 'Your request has not found favour, not with the Goddess Diana, nor Apollo, whom we honour at the Games tomorrow.' She added with force. 'And not with Mars – the God of War!'

Tarquin was horrified. 'But—'

'Legionaries do not beg the gods to guide their hands. They do not plead to win their own little battles. Soldiers of the Second Augustan Legion do not need curses to fight their foes. Fight justly. Fight fairly.'

The young man was shocked. Shaking his head, he said, 'Last time, the old priestess, she placed my curse in front of the statue of the Goddess Diana – inside the temple – it worked.'

In desperation, he looked at her.

'By all the powers, I need the help of the Goddess. I haven't fought in front of so many people before. I—'

He knelt on the steps, pleading with her. 'I – I'm afraid—'

Simone turned away from him and looked towards the hillfort, looming over the fortress. Clouds covered the sun. Shadows raced across the meadow towards the temple.

'You have offended the Goddess. Go from here.'

Stunned, the soldier dropped the lead tablet onto the steps.

'Take this curse. Cast it into the waters of the river; or it will return to you. Cleanse your mind. Cleanse your heart. Cleanse your body. Do not defile the Temple of Diana with a curse. Do **not** return.'

Tarquin picked up the tablet and fled towards the riverbank.

Simone walked slowly back into the temple and stood before the statue.

This is unbelievable! David and Edryn are in the gravest danger. Please – help me to save their lives. I beg you.

Wrapping a shawl tightly around her, she went to search for some kindling.

I must keep the sacred fire alight... then learn the prayers... Tomorrow, I have to find a way to save the boys. And where are Tara and Mariad?

Chapter 9

In the Dungeons

It was late in the afternoon. The storm had passed. Flashes of lightning and rumblings of thunder still echoed around the hills over towards the west.

'How can we get inside the arena?' Tara peered around a timber post by a side entrance. 'There has to be a way to get into the amphitheatre—'

Three slaves with heavy sacks on their shoulders were walking along the track near them.

Mariad hissed. 'Raphael! Come over here.'

A tall young man swivelled around. 'What are you doing here?' He glanced around. 'Go back to the hillfort! If you're caught, you'll be whipped and thrown into the dungeons.'

'But—'

'I can't stop. We need to get these bags of sand

down on the arena before the Games tomorrow.'

'Raphael – this is important.'

Dropping the sack on the ground, he rubbed his shoulder. 'Mariad, I haven't time—'

'We need your help.' Pulling Tara over towards him, she said, 'This is my friend. We're here to find something precious, rare...'

Tara whispered, 'Can we trust him?'

'Yes. Completely. The Romans captured him in Jerusalem, took him to Rome...'

The young man grimaced, and sighed heavily.

'And he rescued Alys, a child of the tribe. She'd wandered off through the woods and down to the fortress. He brought her back. If he hadn't—'

Mariad smiled at him.

He shrugged. 'It was nothing. Anyone would've done the same.'

What sad eyes he has, thought Tara.

'The Seer sent us here on a mission –' said Mariad – 'to find something precious.'

'We must find it,' said Tara. 'If we don't, the Romans will attack the tribe, and everyone in the hillfort will be slaughtered.'

Raphael stood, shaking his head. 'My city, Jerusalem – they destroyed it,' he said. 'I saw terrible things. If I can, I'll help you.'

'You know all the places in the fortress,' said Mariad. 'Where would the Romans hide something rare?'

'What is it?'

'We don't know exactly,' said Tara. 'It was in a riddle. We have to solve it.'

'Something to do with an animal's lair,' added Mariad.

'A lair?' The young man looked puzzled. 'There are no lairs here. All the wild beasts are kept in cages below the arena; bears, wolves, wild boar...' He grimaced. 'You can hear them; howling, crying, growling. They starve them...' He spoke softly. 'So – the riddle – what did it say, exactly?'

'This object – it's for a warrior's hand,' said Mariad.

'It's rare... unique,' said Tara. 'And round.'

'Where would the Romans hide something like that?' asked Mariad.

He pointed over to a building with columns near the riverbank.

'The Temple of Diana. They keep a lot of valuable things there.' He scratched his head. 'Or in the Headquarters – inside the Governor's residence. But that would be impossible. It's heavily guarded.'

'But **you** can go into these places,' said Mariad. 'No one would suspect you – being a slave.'

'That's true.'

'There has to be a way. There has to,' said Tara.

Voices were coming towards them.

'Soldiers! Hide!' muttered Raphael.

The girls slipped behind the post. The slave bent down, pretending to check the sack.

Barely glancing at him, two legionaries strolled

out of a main entrance. One called over to a group of soldiers striding towards the river.

'*Salve!* How goes it?'

'Capilus! Caeso! Have you heard the news?'

'Tell us! We rely on you for all the gossip around here, Lucilius!'

The soldier laughed. 'Tarquin has captured two Silures. Boys. They were stealing gems from the Baths! Can you believe it?'

'No! Really? He's never captured anything in his life! Not even a rabbit!' said Capilus.

'Where are these thieves? In the dungeons?' asked his friend.

'Yes, down there –' Lucilius gestured towards the amphitheatre – 'waiting to be ripped apart by the wild boars!'

'Or the bear...' added his friend.

'That'll be great sport!' grinned Capilus.

'I'd bet on the bear!' said Lucilius.

Laughing, they all walked off together in the direction of the wharf.

The girls exchanged horrified looks.

'The Mirror showed us where they are – in the dungeons...' said Tara.

'What can we do?' asked Mariad.

'You know these boys? Who are they?' asked Raphael.

'One is my brother, my twin,' gulped Tara.

'And the other is Edryn, son of Aled the blacksmith.'

The slave looked gravely at them. 'That's bad. Very bad.'

'How can we save them?' said Mariad.

'Can you help them escape?' said Tara.

'They'll be heavily guarded tonight, and given their last meal. Everyone will go to the dungeons to watch them.'

Oh David. My twin. What have you done? You promised...

'In the morning, they'll be taken up to the arena,' said Raphael. 'There they'll have to fight for their lives.'

Tara fought to stop tears welling up. *Breathe... breathe... I mustn't panic.*

Mariad put her arm around her friend's shoulders and looked at the young man. 'There must be something you can do.'

'No one ever has escaped from the dungeons,' he said. 'After the boys have fought – if they're still alive – the crowd could ask the governor to pardon them. But why would they? The Romans love blood. They're cruel. They enjoy watching people fight, and animals suffer and die. To them it's just a spectacle.'

'There must be a chance,' said Mariad.

Picking up the sack, he slung it over his shoulder.

'I must go. This sand has to be spread over the arena. It's to cover the blood—'

Tara trembled. 'I beg you – my brother... '

'And Edryn – he's a young boy, a bard... The Silures will be forever in your debt... He will sing of your bravery, your courage...'

'I'll try.' He turned away and then back. 'But what about this precious object?'

Tara gripped Mariad's arm. 'First, we must save the boys.'

Her friend nodded. 'I agree.'

'There is one thing...' Raphael shifted the weight of the bag to his other shoulder. 'But you'll need to get inside the amphitheatre. To get in, you must have a token. Slaves sit up in the highest part of the stadium, not in the lower places. The soldiers and merchants sit there.'

'Slaves?' Mariad looked fiery. 'But we're not slaves.'

'That's not the point. You need to look like slaves. Tuck your hair well in under those caps. Watch the entertainment.' He rolled his eyes. 'If you can. Cheer loudly for the boys, so the whole crowd joins in. That sometimes works. It could save their lives. Otherwise—'

'If there's the smallest chance, Raphael...' said Mariad.

'I'll bring some tokens to you later. Where can I find you?'

'Where the track from the hillfort comes out... where you found Alys that day...'

A kingfisher flew onto a branch overhanging the river. At the wharf, the two merchants were watching a line of slaves carrying the last box along the track towards the Customs House.

'Those are valuable pots in there – don't drop even one!' called Blandus. 'And when you get to the courtyard, place them down carefully...'

'Not long till the Games,' Ventus remarked. 'I do enjoy seeing the chariots in the procession. The horses perform so well – and the music – oh, the water organ! Wonderful! What about you?'

'The gladiators always draw me. Although I can't decide who to bet on – Gratius, with his trident and net, or Ativus – he can do damage.'

'Round and round they go.' Ventus yawned. 'I hope it'll be more exciting than the last fight those two had.'

'I heard gladiators from Gaul will be arriving here soon – young men with metal bits in their boxing gloves—'

'They'll be out for blood.'

Neither Ventus nor Blandus noticed a swarthy figure hiding in shadows near the workshops. Listening intently. Stroking a dagger.

'What was the centurion speaking about earlier?' Ventus asked.

Blandus paused. 'The new governor. He'll be issuing his orders soon.'

'Perhaps he'll send the legion to conquer the lands in the north-west, once and for all...'

'Our forts need defending from those Ordivices. Like the Silures – a stone in our boots!'

Ventus brushed some flies from his toga. 'The gold and silver in those hills – it has to get to Rome safely. Or why are we here?'

'Our centurion friend is desperate to attack the tribe here. "If I were the governor, we'd attack them tonight," he said.'

'He might get his wish.'

A slave stumbled as he went past, steadied himself, and balanced the amphora. Walking further along the wharf, he caught sight of the man hiding by the workshops. A finger to the lips. A shake of the head. Staring straight ahead, the slave moved on towards the Customs House.

'Who's this? He's in a hurry,' said Ventus.

A man was running towards the merchants.

'Isn't it the governor's clerk? What does he want?'

'*Salve!* News has just been received of our ships.'

'Yes?'

'Bad news. The worst. This morning, two have been wrecked off the coast.'

'What? Where?'

'On the rocks in the south, near the tin mines. They were bringing grain from Egypt – not only for Isca, but for our fortresses in the north, too.'

'This is a great disappointment,' said Blandus. 'A heavy loss indeed.'

Ventus shrugged. 'Storms, rocks. It's to be expected.'

The clerk bowed and hurried back to the fortress.

'So, there won't be enough grain here in Isca. Interesting.'

'That'll give Linus Paulinus a good reason to raid the Silures hillfort up there and take theirs. This could be the answer to his prayers.'

Blandus snorted. 'I think he prays to Mars, our God of War, every minute of every day!'

'But Julius Frontius would prefer things to stay quiet until he leaves for Rome.'

'His senior centurion might persuade him to give the order.'

The shadows grew longer. The figure slipped away.

A guard came in and placed some bowls on the dungeon floor. 'Your last meal – ever,' he laughed as he went out and locked the metal door.

David eyed the bowls in front of them.

'This looks like a little body. Is it a tiny chicken?' He poked it. 'Strange. It's covered in honey and nuts. Smells good!'

Edryn was trembling in the corner of the dungeon.

'How can you think about food?' he cried. 'Tomorrow, we're going to die!'

He's right. And this is all my fault. So I need to work out how we can escape from here.

Two gladiators were sitting in a chamber next to theirs. Between them were thick metal bars.

One was sharpening the prongs of his trident. 'All three as sharp as crocodile's teeth! Cut straight through anything now. Perfect!' He peered at the boys. 'So, why are you two here?'

'Just visiting?' asked the other as he mended his net.

David sighed. 'We were in the Baths, looking at gems that'd been dropped at the bottom of the pool. A soldier accused us of stealing them.'

'It wasn't true,' added Edryn.

The men chuckled.

'That doesn't make any difference to the Romans. The more slaves to throw into the arena, the better.'

'Great entertainment!'

Edryn turned his face to the wall and moaned quietly.

'Where are you from?' asked David.

'Priscus here is from Macedonia. My name's Decimus. I'm from North Africa. We're here for the money – and our freedom.'

Perhaps we could learn something useful for tomorrow... how to survive in the arena, thought David.

'Have you been a gladiator long?' he asked.

'Eight years now. Two more and, if I live, I'll be free,' said Priscus. 'I'd go to Londinium then. More action there. Or Rome.'

'Pass over that dormouse,' said Decimus, 'and I might go easy on you two tomorrow. A quick death.'

'A dormouse?' David was holding the mammal by its tail. 'Ergh! Have it,' he said as he pushed the little body through the bars.

A gulp. It was gone.

'Tasty!'

Edryn stared at the man's muscles.

'We have to fight **you**?'

'Fight? I wouldn't call it that!' Decimus grinned. 'What can you do against me? Headbutt my arm!'

Roaring with laughter, the gladiator thrust his head up to the bars.

Edryn cowered, pressing himself further into the wall.

'Don't take any notice of him,' said Priscus. 'You'll be fighting the animals. Maybe the bear. He's angry. None of them have had any food for days. They're famished.'

'What a spectacle it'll be!' said Decimus. 'The crowd loves watching a slave – or a thief – being ripped apart.'

I think I'm going to be sick, thought David.

Edryn gripped his friend's arm. 'What are we going to do?'

Decimus grinned at them. 'Don't worry. It'll be quick.'

'We'll be on after they've taken your bodies away,' said Priscus, examining his net for holes.

Silence.

'Hey, Decimus. Who will the crowd shout for tomorrow? You or me?'

'We'll put on a good show for them. Like always.'

'We will, won't we?'

Priscus nudged his friend. 'Him with the iron ball and hammer. and me with trident and net. Grr!'

'Argh!' Decimus growled.

'You'd kill each other?' said David, astonished.

'Not unless we're given the order. The people like to see us gouging eyes out.'

'Thumbs up and one dies. Thumbs down, we live.'

'I thought it's the other way around,' said David, thinking of the films he'd seen.

'You thought wrong. Better get it right, or you'll be dead before you know it!'

All was quiet in the hillfort.

Dreaming she was, the Seer. Dreaming of galaxies; spiralling, twisting. Of the birth of the planet, she dreamt... *Volcanoes erupting, lava flowing, crystals growing; purple clusters, threads of red...* In her hands, a crystal. A wand; purple, long, thin, pointed.

O Amethyst Wand
As this Planet spins,
O Wand of Balance.
A new era begins.

O Amethyst Wand
Reveal the truth,
O Wand of Protection.
Give this message to the youth.

For this planet to heal.
There must be peace,
Battles must stop
Wars must cease.

To you, the word is given,
O Warriors of New Earth,
To you the word is sent,
At this time of birth.

Care for all animals,
Save the bees,
Cleanse the oceans
Plant more trees.

For this planet to live,
For this world to flourish,

All must live in truth,
All must have courage.

O Amethyst Wand,
It is time to choose —
To love — to protect Nature,
Or lose... lose... lose...

The Seer trembled. As she came out of the trance, she looked up to the Heavens.

The moon has risen. Soon it will be full. The time travellers are in great peril.... They must not fail in their task... they must not...

Edryn had curled himself up into a ball and was facing the wall.

Soldiers, merchants, people inside and outside the fortress, had come to watch the prisoners eat their last meal.

Pheasant brains, pigs' udders and fish livers had been laid out on the dungeon floor.

The boys had refused to eat, speak, or even look at anyone.

'This is disappointing!'
'Go on! Eat those udders! Delicious!'
'Entertain us!'

'Sing!'

'You Silures like singing.'

The stonemason almost choked at the stench. 'It's filthy in here – ugh! It reeks!'

'And so hot!'

'Let's just go.'

After they were left alone, David began running around in a circle. Then he did some press-ups.

'What are you doing, David?'

'Preparing for tomorrow. Doing these exercises might help – to run away from the animals. Boars can be tricky.'

'They're bound to catch us,' said Edryn. 'Then they'll gore us with their tusks. We're going to die.'

Later that night, the gladiators were snoring loudly and calling out in their sleep.

David whispered. 'Are you awake, Edryn?'

'Yes.'

'I'm sorry. This is all my fault. If we hadn't gone into the Baths...'

The young boy choked back tears. 'And if you hadn't dived for those gemstones.'

'I know. But it's no use thinking of the past. Let's make a plan, Edryn.'

'To escape from here? It's impossible.'

'You're right. Too many guards,' muttered David. 'It's called – self-help – we need to think positive. We have to work out how we're going to live...'

'I don't think we're going to.'

Chapter 10

Let the Games Begin!

All night, Simone had been awake, learning the prayers and the rituals for the Games. The morning light grew brighter as she stood in front of the statue of Diana.

'I beg you, O Goddess: Help me to perform the rituals perfectly. Help me to save David and Edryn – and help all of us to find the talisman – whatever it is – and take it to the Seer. Forgive me for throwing the nail into the river.'

Tears filled her eyes.

No. Stop crying. It's time to dig deep. You can do this.

Earlier, she had found more robes, and had chosen a long blue one.

Priestesses braid their hair. I'll use these ribbons

– blue, yellow... Now, I must remember to take the cakes for the ritual. Pour oil – is that before or after I bow to the statue of Nemesis? This is so difficult. But somehow I have to save David and Edryn.

Footsteps crunched on the path outside the temple and stopped. The guards had arrived.

When in doubt – look calm, breathe, look confident. Be Cleopatra!

At the bottom of the wide steps, two soldiers stood. They bowed.

'We have come to escort you to the amphitheatre, Priestess.'

'To the games honouring Apollo.'

The girls had woken before dawn and were hurrying across the meadow to the amphitheatre. Having pushed her leather cap firmly down on her head, Tara handed the wooden tokens to the soldier.

'Slaves – up the top.'

Clambering up the steps to the highest place in the stands, the girls took their seats.

'We can see everything from here,' said Mariad, gazing down on the arena.

I don't want to see everything. Tara remembered

films about gladiators fighting to the death with swords and daggers, tridents and nets.

That was fake blood. This will be real. And today it could be my brother's.

Below, the tiers around the arena were filling up. Soldiers called to each other, joking, laughing, placing bets.

'Is Priscus on today?'

'I've a bet on Decimus.'

'You've wasted your money!'

The sun rose higher. Beads of sweat began to trickle down Tara's cheeks.

When will they bring David on? Will they make him fight bears? Wild boar?

'O Goddess, I beg you, protect my twin,' she whispered. 'Protect Edryn.'

Mariad clasped her hand. 'If we can find a way to save them, we will. I swear it.'

As Simone was carried in a litter along the track by the side of the fort, she glanced at the South Gate to her left. Over to her right was the amphitheatre.

Shouts and loud calls were already coming from there.

Oh! I'm dreading this. Soon, they'll be dragging

David and Edryn into the arena. They'll have to fight for their lives. What can I do?

She shivered. *I must find a way of saving them.*

The soldiers conducted Simone to her box. Beneath her was the shrine of Nemesis.

At the top of the stand opposite, something caught her eye; two figures.

One stood up and was pulled back down.

Can it be Tara? And Mariad?

We must get together somehow, and save the boys.

She took a deep breath. *Don't panic. Be calm.*

A flurry around her; the governor was arriving.

As he took his seat in the box next to hers, he smiled and bowed.

She inclined her head; a little.

This feels like a dream. A nightmare. Let it end!

A trumpet sounded. She turned towards the entrance. *It begins.*

Leading the procession was the standard-bearer. Next came the trumpeters, followed by a band of horn-players. Cohorts marched in, and finally, accompanied by a great fanfare, the gladiators. The crowd jumped up, cheering and clapping.

The first, tall, dark-haired and broad-shouldered, carried a trident, net and dagger.

Quickly joining him was a stocky, fair-haired fighter, holding a metal ball and a spiked, round hammer. He glowered at the spectators.

Another gladiator, his head covered by a

gleaming bronze helmet, held up a sword, waved it around, and roared.

Behind him, gladiators paraded from every part of the Empire: tall, black Ethiopians; short, olive-skinned Macedonians; pale, stocky Gauls. All were holding their weapons ready; swords, daggers, shields, javelins, scimitars. All ready to maim and to kill.

Simone trembled.

Will David and Edryn have to fight these men? What hope have they got?

The gladiators were now standing in a line in front of the governor's box.

Tiberius Blandus leant over towards the governor. 'Great news from Rome – we hear the most magnificent amphitheatre in the Empire is almost completed.'

'They used the treasure found in the temple in Jerusalem,' added Ventus.

'Statues of the Gods all around. The Flavian Arena, they're calling it, after our emperor and his son.'

'How splendid to spend all the treasure from Judea on that,' said Ventus.

'Watch where you are putting those olives!' Blandus frowned at a slave who had slipped and almost tipped a tray over him. 'Clumsy idiot!'

The governor fixed his gaze straight ahead.

'Thousands of wild beasts are being brought from all across the Empire. 100 days of slaughter a year!' continued the merchant. 'Imagine! Lions, tigers, crocodiles, giraffes, and those river horses – what are they called?'

'Hippopotamuses,' replied his friend.

'All from our conquered lands,' said Blandus. 'What a sight! I'd like to be there!' He surveyed the stadium. 'Really, this amphitheatre should be built of stone. This timber won't last many winters here. A canvas roof to keep out the rain in this damp country would be good.'

Julius Frontius adjusted his toga and sighed. 'Yes, yes. However, we are not in Rome. These Games provide quite enough entertainment for the legion here.'

'We could stage more of a spectacle though, sir,' said Linus Paulinus. 'I could train the soldiers to slay leopards and many other wild beasts...' His eyes glazed over. 'When I was in Verona—'

The governor said sternly, 'There is much work to be done in the months – or weeks – before I leave for Rome. Designing a better drainage system to stop the meadows flooding here. That's more important than teaching the men to kill wild beasts.'

The centurion swallowed hard. 'Yes, sir.'

Glancing around the arena, Julius Frontius said, 'All is ready. Let's begin.'

He turned to Simone. 'Priestess. May we ask you to give the blessing on these Games: in honour of the god, Apollo.' To the centurion, he said, 'Escort the priestess to the shrine of Nemesis.'

Standing in front of the shrine, clutching the sacred cakes tightly, Simone declared, 'Nemesis, Goddess of Fate and Divine Vengeance. Punisher of crimes. Source of Justice. On this sacred day, we honour you, together with the God, Apollo.'

After crumbling the cakes, she hesitated.

A slave standing behind her whispered, 'Here's the jar, pour the oil all over the offering.'

Taking the glass flask, she tipped the oil over the crumbs. The crowd clapped and cheered.

Now – walk, shoulders back. Look like a priestess; graceful, dignified.

She looked back to catch a glimpse of the slave, but he had disappeared.

Taking her seat in the box once more, she breathed deeply.

The centurion spoke: 'Sir. May we request that you say some words?'

Adjusting his toga, Julius Frontius stood; the crowd were ready to explode with excitement.

'We are here today, in Britannia, in Isca, at the furthest outpost of our great Roman Empire.'

There was a hush.

'To bring *Pax Romana,* the peace of Rome, to these wild, barbaric lands. In the name of our emperor, Vespasian, and those before him. We have conquered many tribes. Our Empire, the mightiest in the world, embraces all peoples, all races, all beliefs. Bow to Rome and all are equal.'

Simone sat still.

What about women? They're not equal. Nor the thousands of slaves.

'Rome! The greatest power the world has ever seen! Or will see. Nothing can stand in our way; not the tribes of Britannia, nor Nature itself – it must bow to us. We need straight roads, so we cut down forest, upon forest... This we must do! For mighty Rome!'

The people cheered.

Simone twisted her fingers, round and round, as the governor spoke of drains, pipes, concrete.

She tried not to listen. *Is this where it all started?* she thought. *Destroying forests where animals live... sacred places...*

The governor sat down, to great applause.

The centurion coughed.

'Ah, yes.' He rose again, looked around the stadium, and declared: 'The Roman Empire will live for a thousand years!'

'For two thousand!'

'Forever!'

No, it won't.

'Long live Vespasian, Emperor of Rome!'

Cheering came from all around the arena, from the highest tiers to the boxes.

Julius Frontius took a cup of wine from a slave, held it up and said, 'Let the games begin!'

Six thousand soldiers, merchants and tradesmen applauded, on and on.

Simone closed her eyes. *I'm not here. I'm sitting by a trickling stream, in the shade of beautiful trees. Birds are singing... I'm going for a walk with the twins and Bethan along the riverbank. To be anywhere but here...*

Yet the cries of the animals, the sound of clashing swords, the blare of the horns, the screeching notes from the organ, never stopped. She wanted to block out the noise. *Let it stop. Let it stop!*

'Priestess?' A slave was offering her a tray of pastries; she shook her head.

The scent of incense, frankincense and myrrh, wafted towards her.

But it couldn't mask the putrid smell of blood. Over and over, the sand was raked. To cover the flesh; to cover the blood.

Dark red stains remained. She couldn't look. She couldn't watch.

She half opened her eyes. The centurion was standing up.

'Now is the time for – the hunting of the animals!'

The stadium erupted.

'We have a new young gladiator today. But,' he laughed, 'perhaps this is his very last day!'

Shouting. Calling. Trumpets blaring.

Simone blinked and stared at the entrance opposite; there was her cousin.

An official walked over towards him. 'Here, slave. Take this *gladius*!'

A short sword was thrust into David's hand. He dropped it onto the sand.

'What's he doing?'

'Not doing!'

Laughter rippled along the tiers.

'Stand and fight! Be a warrior!' shouted a voice from the stands.

'Coward!'

'Here is Davidus, a common thief,' declared Linus Paulinus. 'A barbarian. How will you fare against these wild beasts? O stealer of gems!'

David strode into the centre of the arena; he faced the shrine of Nemesis. He had no sword, no dagger, no trident. How was he going to defend himself?

He glanced up towards the governor's box and saw Simone. Astonished, he took a step back.

She nodded, not listening to the chatter of the merchants in the nearby boxes.

'What do you think his chances of survival are?'

'Nil!'

Simone dug her nails into her palms. Stealing a glance around, she wondered if Tara and Mariad had come down, closer to the arena.

How can we save David? Maybe they'll let him go....

A roar.

Into the arena hurtled a wolf. Fangs bared; yellow eyes burning. He circled the boy, danced towards him, away from him, getting ready to pounce.

'Tear him apart!'

'Rip his eyes out!'

David stood still. He did not run. Neither did he look into the eyes of the wolf.

Slowly, he knelt down on the sanded ground and patted it.

'Good boy,' he whispered. 'There's a good boy.'

The wolf stopped, put his head to one side, and stared at him.

The spectators were astounded.

'What's he doing – kneeling down?'

'He's giving up!'

'No fun in that!'

'Stand and fight, thief!'

The crowd began to encourage the animal as it gave a series of low growls.

'Come on! Rip his hand off!'

'Sink your teeth into his leg!'

'Tear him limb from limb!'

Speaking softly, David said, 'It's fine. I'm not going to hurt you.' He paused. 'And you aren't going to hurt me, either, are you?'

The crowd was stunned. Some began to call out.

'Go for his liver!'

'Eat his entrails!'

The wolf snarled. His teeth bared. His eyes flamed.

Simone was terrified. *What can I do? This wild beast will kill him. O Goddess, I beg you, protect him.*

Inch by inch, David stretched out his hand, his palm facing downwards.

Growling, snarling, the wolf moved nearer. Then he sniffed David's fingers, and touched the tips with his wet nose.

'Bite his arm off!'

'He's a thief!'

'Traitor!'

Keeping his hand straight, David continued to whisper to the wolf.

The animal whined a little, licked the boy's knuckles, sat, turned his head sideways, and looked deep into his eyes.

'Good boy,' said David. 'I'm going to stroke your head now. Is that alright?' David ran his hand gently over the wolf's head. 'That's right. There's a good boy.'

The wolf edged up closer to him, and began to nuzzle his chin.

'Sorcery!' came a shout.

The centurion leapt up, roaring, 'Get that beast – that wolf – out of here – now!'

A slave ran forward, grabbed the wolf around its neck, and dragged the now-tamed animal away.

Jeers echoed around the stadium.

'Rubbish!'

'Pathetic!'

'Give us some action!'

As he shielded his eyes from the sun, David caught sight of Tara and Mariad sitting up at the top of the stadium. His sister had her head in her hands. He glanced at Simone, who was staring straight ahead.

Why is Simone sitting with the Romans? What happens now? I'm not out of trouble yet. Edryn's still in the dungeons. I need to get him out...

'That was excellent. We should get him to train our hunting dogs,' said the governor. 'Perhaps –' he turned towards Simone – 'a pardon could be given?'

Before she could answer, a young soldier marched into the arena. Giving a quick bow to the governor, he shouted, 'May I have your permission to fight this thief, this liar, this traitor, sir?'

In his hand he held a clay tablet. He glared at Simone.

The curse! He didn't throw it into the river.

The crowd screamed.

'It's Tarquin!'

'Give us a proper fight!'

'Kill the thief!'

Julius Frontius waved his hand at the soldier. 'If you must – er —'

'Gaius Tarquin Livinius,' said the centurion. 'Not one of our best, sir.'

The governor nodded. 'Let the fight begin.'

Tarquin placed the tablet at the shrine of Nemesis.

The merchants began to mutter amongst themselves.

'What's he doing, Blandus?'

'Looks like a curse to me…'

'Oh, what? Really? Fight fair.'

The young soldier took his sword from his scabbard, and stood glowering at his enemy.

'I will now cut this runaway slave to tiny ribbons with my *gladius*!'

He waved it around as he scowled at the crowd. 'I have done such deeds with these!'

Simone closed her eyes. *Don't look. Don't show you are frightened.*

Roars filled the stadium.

'Start the fight!'

'Fight? One with weapons – the other with none?'

'Won't last long…'

Linus Paulinus turned to the governor. 'I heard he used a curse the last time he fought, sir.'

'Make this a fair fight, soldier,' ordered Julius Frontius. 'Throw away your weapons.'

Tarquin froze. 'But—'

'Now!'

Furious, Tarquin threw his dagger and sword down onto the sand.

The band continued to play; slaves passed around trays of cakes, pastries, dates, and cups of wine.

Standing in the centre of the arena, the young legionary shouted, 'I'll defeat this wild barbarian with my bare hands! I don't need a *pugio* or a *gladius*.'

'Or a curse!' came a shout, followed by laughter.

'I, Gaius Tarquin Livinius, have the protection of Nemesis!'

'Oh. Listen to him!'

'The Goddess of Fate herself is looking after him!'

'O Fortunate one!'

The governor turned to the centurion. 'Pass the order down. Remove the curse from the shrine.'

'Now we'll have a contest!'

'You're on your own, Tarquin!'

Laughter could be heard above the music.

The young soldier hesitated, then turned, faced his opponent and spat. 'Silures thief!'

David could feel anger welling up inside. His eyes narrowed as he glared at his enemy.

A whisper came:

Do not show your anger. If you allow his words to stir up your feelings, you will always be controlled by him... Always.

David gritted his teeth as he watched his enemy circle him.

Traveller through time and space. Remember the wars you fought in on many planets? Remember – the blood you spilled? Remember – your punishment? Banishment to deep space for aeons. Do you wish to repeat that? To be alone. To freeze. Forever, forever...

An image flashed into David's mind; a planet covered in deep snow and thick ice. Alone, shivering on a mountain peak. Solitary. No night;

162

no day. Time passed so very slowly there.

I can control my feelings... I can... I must...

As the young soldier moved towards him, David took a few steps back.

'Afraid to stand and fight, barbarian?'

Tarquin kept throwing insults and taunting him. 'Coward! Savage!'

Keep your distance. Wait. Patience. Wait for him to move first.

And he did. Tarquin leapt forward and threw himself on his foe.

David ducked, catching him around the waist. He felt blows flailing on his shoulders and arms, but he held on tightly. Throwing Tarquin onto his back, he pinned him down. Then, bending his knees, David used his legs to keep him flat on his back on the ground. Tarquin wriggled and squirmed, trying to land even one blow. But he couldn't.

'Let me go, you thief!'

In the next second, David had turned his enemy onto his front, his face close to the sand. He clasped his arms around Tarquin's middle, forcing him down once. And down again; his cheek was on the ground.

'I – I—'

'Davidus! Davidus!' The crowd exploded.

'What a hero!' they shouted.

'A warrior!'

'How did he do that?'

'Truly amazing!'

David stood up, brushed off the sand, and bowed to the governor.

While the crowd were clapping and cheering, others were jeering at the defeated soldier.

'Tarquin the Vanquished!'

'Let's have the gladiators on – they're real fighters!'

The young legionary stood up shakily, wiped the sand off his face, and staggered out of the arena.

An arm purse landed at David's feet.

Picking it up, he felt the coins inside, and waved to the spectators.

'Freedom for Davidus!' they shouted.

'Pardon him!'

'In honour of Apollo!'

The governor leant towards Simone.

'Priestess – may you grant a pardon—?'

He stopped. A chariot, driven at full speed, thundered into the arena. There, holding the reins with one hand and waving a whip with the other, was Tarquin, his face on fire.

The soldier drove the horses straight towards David. There was uproar.

David had his back to the chariot but, on hearing the sound of hooves, he swivelled around. Two horses were galloping towards him.

The band continued to play above the screaming and shouting.

At first, it seemed that David was going to be mown down by the horses and caught under the chariot's wheels. Certain death.

Tarquin was leaning over the side, his whip raised, ready to strike at David's head.

Everything began to move in slow motion. David moved sideways. A wheel came loose, and spun off. The horses reared up, flinging Tarquin to the ground.

He lay there, motionless.

'Davidus! Davidus!' were the cries.

Two slaves came running over with a stretcher, while others caught and calmed the horses. Everyone was on their feet, shouting.

'Did you see that?'

'Impressive!'

Tarquin was lifted onto the stretcher. Was he alive? Or dead? He raised his left arm.

'Mercy,' he moaned.

The noise was overwhelming.

'May we pardon Gaius Tarquin Livinius, sir?' said the centurion. 'It's too much trouble to do anything else with him. I shall give him enough punishments to last the next two decades.'

Julius Frontius nodded. 'Send him to Caledonia, to Julius Agricola. He can fight the barbarian tribes of the north.'

He called to the slaves. 'Let him be taken to the hospital. Tend his wounds.'

Leaning over towards Simone, he said, 'And as for the victor?'

She inclined her head.

'Excellent. We give thanks to Apollo.' He gestured towards David. 'Would you like to pardon him now?'

Simone stood up and, looking over her cousin's head, announced, 'Davidus, at these Games, held in honour of the god Apollo, you are the victor! He, with his sister, the goddess Diana, grants you pardon.'

Her eyes flickered down to him; he stood in the middle of the arena, trying not to grin.

'Before the sun sets, you must give thanks this day at the Temple of Diana.'

David bowed. *Awesome! She must have seen loads of films about the Roman Empire! What a natural!*

'Er – Priestess. May I ask pardon for my brother Edry – Eddidus. He is in the dungeons, and is innocent of any crime.'

Before the governor could answer, Simone declared, 'Both have been pardoned, Davidus and Eddidus.' She raised her voice. 'Make haste to the Temple of Diana.'

I hope Tara and Mariad can hear me, she thought.

Simone turned to the governor. 'My duties here are complete. The sacred fire at the temple must be tended.'

The governor smiled as the assistant priestess left the stadium.

Chapter 11

News from Rome!

From the top tiers to the bottom, the spectators were whistling, shouting and clapping, while David smiled and waved to them.

Tara groaned.

Twin! Listen! Get out of the stadium now! Get Edryn. Run to the Temple of Diana. We'll meet you there. Go!

Her twin continued bowing to everyone; in the north stands, the south, east and west.

Any minute now, he'll be blowing them kisses. Oh, my brother!

'Let's go!' Mariad tugged at her arm, and they began walking down the wooden steps.

'Wait!

Something on the river had caught Tara's eye.

'What's that?'

Coming around the curve of the bend, making for the quay, was a huge ship.

Oars were up, the gangway was about to be thrown down. A figure leapt onto the riverbank.

Clutching something to his chest, he called to a group of slaves working by the wharf. One pointed towards the amphitheatre.

'Let's wait a little longer, Mariad. This looks important.'

The audience was still praising David when the messenger burst into the arena.

Racing over to the governor's box, he knelt, bowed his head, and offered him a scroll.

Silence.

Julius Frontius unrolled the papyrus. Whispers began to fly around the stadium.

'That ship's from Ostia.'

'News from Rome?'

'Another great victory.'

More figs and pistachios!'

'More soldiers to crush the Silures?'

The governor stood, raising his hand for silence.

'Men of the Second Augustan Legion,' he began, 'there is news from Rome.'

He took a deep breath.

'Our great emperor, Vespasian – he is with the gods.'

There was silence, followed by cries and mutterings throughout the stadium.

'The emperor's dead.'

'How did he die?'

'Poisoned like Claudius?'

'Killed himself?'

'Nero did that.'

'Or, as Caesar was – betrayed and stabbed?'

The centurion glared down at David. Had he known that the Emperor was going to die?

The governor continued reading, 'During his reign, mighty deeds were accomplished –' listing them all, he ended – 'and the Jews of Judea were crushed.'

He looked up to the cloudless sky. 'May the gods welcome Vespasian into their realm. Hail Vespasian!'

The crowd roared. 'All hail Vespasian!'

'Now he's with the gods. We honour him.'

David stood still. *What should I do now?*

The band readied themselves to herald the new emperor. Julius Frontius paused.

'Our new emperor is –' The trumpeters blew their horns – 'Titus. Son of Vespasian...'

Loud cheers drowned his words.

'Hail Titus! Emperor of the glorious Roman Empire!'

'Conqueror of Judea...'

Raising his hand once more, the governor gave the scroll to his scribe.

Silence fell.

'Legionaries – a new era begins. Let the Games

continue in honour of Apollo. And – our new emperor – Titus.'

'Titus! Titus!'

Applause and clapping came from all around the stadium. Tara covered her ears as the water organ struck up, trumpeters blew their horns, percussionists hit their instruments.

David stared up at the stands. He could see Tara and Mariad hurrying down the steps.

All was confusion as the spectators discussed the news and the cohorts paraded around the arena.

Tara arrived at a side entrance and swivelled around. David hadn't moved.

Twin! Will you listen to me! Leave with Edryn this second. Meet us at the Temple of Diana. Move! Go! Now!

David raced through the dimly lit passages.

Sounds of crying, of whimpering, were coming from the cages. He peered into the darkness. The young bear was clawing at the bars of her cage. Next to her was the wolf, licking his wounds.

What can I do? David looked into the eyes of the bear.

I am suffering here, he heard. *Please release me – and my friends. We won't harm you.*

'I'm going to let you all out.'

As he opened the cage, he felt sick; the stench was overpowering.

'Go towards the trees on the hill.'

The bear shuffled forwards, squeezed David's

hand, and waddled down the passage.

Then David pulled at the catch on the wolf's cage. One tug and the metal door opened. The wolf nuzzled David's leg and padded off.

Freedom!

'David! Is that you?'

'Edryn! I just have to do something—'

As he unlocked the third cage, the boar charged past him.

Staggering back, David thought, *I hope that was a good idea.*

He felt his way along the wall. Here, it was darker.

'Where are you?'

'Here – there aren't any torches. I'm just moving along a bit.'

David touched metal bars. A key was in the lock. As he swung the door open he whispered, 'Let's get out of here – quickly!'

David untied the ropes around his friend's wrists.

'What's happening? The guards told me I was next. Then suddenly they all disappeared.'

'They're in the arena.'

Edryn grasped David's arm. 'Am I going to face the bear? I'll just be a mouthful, they said, and laughed at me.'

'We're free. We've been pardoned.'

'Truly?'

'Simone did it.'

'Simone?' The boy gasped. 'How?'

'We'll find out later. And they've a new emperor. They'll be celebrating for hours. Which is the quickest way out? We're meeting the girls at the Temple of Diana.

'Down here. But we must free the animals.'

'Done it! Come on. Run!'

'Bring cabbage, ham and sausages,' said the governor to the slave. 'And tell the scribe I wish to see him.'

'Will you be returning to the Games this afternoon, sir?' asked the centurion.

'No. I need to write a report for our new emperor. It must be sent on the next tide.'

'Will there be changes?'

'There are always changes, Linus Paulinus. To live is to change.'

'Yes, sir.' The centurion sighed. *He has these sayings. But I'm never sure what they mean.*

'If you can wait until the scribe comes...'

'Sir.'

I wonder why he wants me to wait, thought Linus Paulinus.

Glancing around at the statues of emperors, his eyes alighted on Claudius.

*The first to invade Britain. After him, Nero –
completely mad, of course. To disagree with him
meant instant death. Then Vespasian. Now, Titus.*
He grinned. *My leader when we destroyed the
temple in Jerusalem and razed the city to the
ground.* He stared out into the courtyard. *New
coins. New orders. New battles to fight?*

Julius Frontius continued drawing. 'Have I
shown you this aqueduct I'm designing?'

'Where will it be, sir?'

'Possibly Rome. Who can tell?' He shrugged. 'I
was to return to Rome. Titus may send me back to
Gaul.'

The centurion's eyes gleamed.

The governor looked up at this rough soldier. *He
would prefer to be in the arena, watching
gladiators fight each other to the death.*

'There's no need for you to remain here. Tell the
men they can stay to see the afternoon's sport.
Boxing? Wrestling? I don't need the guards here,
either.'

'But what about that boy, the one who defeated
Gaius Tarquin Livinius?'

'What about him?'

'A Silures – he could be intent on killing you, sir.
And the wills and documents – the Legion's money
– it's all in the vault below. As well as—'

They exchanged looks.

'It is still there. Safe.'

The governor pushed his drawings away. 'He's

just a boy. And besides, he's been pardoned. No, we've seen the last of him. Why would he come here?' He smiled. 'When she returns, I will ask Livia, the Priestess, to conduct a ritual. All will be well.'

Simone walked with elegance up the temple steps, past the columns, and into the atrium. She smiled as she took off the veil and threw it over the couch.

I could get used to this, All I have to do is to tend the fire here... Oh! The fire!

She rushed over to it. The embers were only just glowing.

I must find some twigs.

Turning, she saw two boys standing in front of her, grinning, both holding some kindling.

'David! Edryn!'

'Davidus to you!' He bowed deeply. 'I thank you for the pardon!'

Edryn placed the pieces of wood by the sacred fire.

'I'll put some on now.' Simone bent down so they couldn't see her eyes were wet.

'I was terrified when they let the wolf in,' she said as she picked up some twigs. 'I thought he was going to kill you.'

'My animal spirit is a wolf. I knew it'd be fine.'

'Animal spirit?' Simone was puzzled.

'Everyone is given the spirit of an animal. It helps us; it guides us through our lives. Mine's a wolf.'

'I wonder what mine is?'

'Hi! Hello!' Voices came from a side chamber.

'Tara!'

'Mariad!'

'Wow! The team is back,' said David. 'Epic!'

'*Bene!*' Simone clapped her hands.

'Where have you been, Mariad?' asked Edryn.

'In the stadium. We watched David taming the wolf,' she said.

Tara smiled at her twin. 'Your display of martial arts was truly awesome!'

David grinned. 'I know.'

The Goddess helped you. Don't get all boastful! OK.

He turned to his cousin. 'Do you think wolf whispering and martial arts will catch on with the Romans?'

'*No!*' They are brutal! They love blood. Conquest. Power. *Et mort.* And death. *Multo morte.* So much death.' Simone trembled.

Tara and David stared at her. *What's happened to our cuz? She's changed.*

'Tell us about the precious object. Have you found it yet?' asked Edryn.

Tarquin lay on a stretcher, battered and bruised. His helmet, armour and belt were lying on the floor, next to his sword and dagger.

'My honour! My honour!' he shouted as he thrashed around. Sweat rolled down his face.

A slave was putting a poultice on his leg.

'Where am I? Are you trying to poison me?'

'You're in the hospital. I've mixed some herbs. They'll help to heal this wound quickly.' *And calm you,* he added as he crushed some more lavender with sprigs of rosemary and sage.

Tarquin stared around the room. A collection of long metal hooks was lined up on the table: saws, and scalpels.

'Don't touch me! Don't cut off my leg!'

'Stay still. I must put this poultice on. If this wound gets infected—'

'O my head. My head! It pains me.'

A headache... If I had a sting ray to put on it, that would help. But we haven't any here...

Tarquin groaned. 'What happened? I – Argh! You're hurting me.'

The slave stepped back. 'You rode a chariot into the arena. When you fell, you hit your head on the ground.' He paused. 'Now, don't move. I have to clean all this blood off.'

The soldier squirmed as the slave dabbed at the wound.

'If I die – I'll have you flogged.'

The slave rolled his eyes. 'You have a cut on your elbow... I'll put some herbs on this too, but first—'

'He pierced me – with a *gladius.*' Tarquin pointed to his heart. 'He stabbed me here! And here!'

'Keep still. He had no *gladius.* He didn't stab you.'

'Don't talk to me like that – I will have you whipped – Argh!'

'I need to cover this wound with a dressing.'

'No. I must go.' The young soldier tried to climb off the stretcher. 'I have to find him. Where's my sword...? I can't see... I'm blind!'

'I've made a potion for you. Drink it. And you need to rest.'

'Poison!' Tarquin raved on. 'You're giving me poison! You want to kill me!'

He fell off the stretcher onto his knees and clutched at the slave's tunic.

'Blood. Oh, so much blood – from such a small body,' he whimpered.

'You have lost very little blood. Drink this. It's fennel. It'll calm you.'

The slave helped him back onto the stretcher, and put the cup to his lips.

'Sip slowly.'

'Her blood. **Her** blood. I'm a soldier. I had to kill her. I had to. A child. A little girl...' He sobbed.

'She offered me water. I stabbed her. I killed her.'
He moaned as he pushed the drink aside and
continued to weep. 'They will avenge us.'

'Who?'

'The Silures.' He waved his hand around. 'The
savages up there. No peace. No peace... Not for me.
Never... The gods – they will never forgive me...'

The soldier fell into a deep sleep as the slave
thought about the secret he'd discovered.

'Can I say that I'm famished? I am so hungry?' said
David, picking up a bowl of grapes.

'We had porridge for breakfast.'

'But that was hours ago, Edryn.'

'They gave us a feast last night because we were
going to die.' The young boy shuddered. 'I couldn't
eat anything. The dormouse...'

David made a face at his friend.

'You ate a mouse?' Simone was horrified.

'Covered in honey and nuts they were,' said
Edryn.

Tara threw The Look at her twin.

'I didn't eat it! I gave it to one of the gladiators,'
said David quickly.

Mariad looked around the atrium. 'Where are the
priestesses?'

Simone looked at the floor. 'Er – I don't know.'

David sent a mind-message to his sister: *She's hiding something, Twin.*

I know, but what? We need to find out.

You try.

'So, cuz,' said David, 'what have you been doing since we last saw you?' He popped an olive into his mouth. 'Blow by blow account. Leave nothing out.'

'After I –' she began – 'then I...'

'Buried the nail by the East Gate?' suggested David. 'Said the words?'

'Yes, that.' She hesitated. 'I – I was standing by the riverbank and noticed this temple. It looks exactly like one – er –' she glanced at Mariad – 'where I live. So I came in, saw these clothes and put them on. Aren't they beautiful?'

Tara threw her cousin The Look.

'Only as a disguise. But the priestess hadn't come back – from er – somewhere... Burr—'

'Newsflash!' said David. 'Priestess abducted by aliens!'

Simone stroked the robe. 'Feel this – it's so much nicer to wear than that itchy tunic.' She half glanced at Tara and tossed her head. 'Anyway, I thought – why not? So I bathed and changed into these.'

David leaned towards her. 'What do you think of the oils?' he asked. 'I tried some in the Baths. The lavender is...'

'So that's how you boys got caught,' said Tara.

'Finish your story, cuz. said David hurriedly. 'Then we need to hear the second riddle.'

Taking a breath, Simone gabbled, 'The governor sent soldiers to escort the Priestess Livia from the temple to his quarters. She wasn't here, so I went instead. She's in Blestium, Burr – somewhere. So he asked me to conduct the rituals at the Games.'

Edryn gasped. 'No!'

'What's the matter?' She looked around at the group. 'It was the only thing I could think of doing. And I had to stay up all night, learning the prayers and all the rituals. So tiring.' She yawned.

'But why were you standing by the river?' asked Mariad. 'You should've been by the East Gate.'

'We saw the soldiers and we thought you were being arrested,' added Tara.

'I was watching the birds. They're different from er – home. The colours – er—'

'What?' David's eyes widened. He mind-messaged his twin. *She's not telling the truth...*

I know.

Birds are either big or small, blue or red to her. But why? Why is she telling lies?

Simone glanced down at her robe and began pulling at the white threads.

'So, shouldn't we all be looking for the talisman now?'

'Yes! Tell us what the second riddle is,' said Edryn.

Tara closed her eyes and repeated the words.

Seek that which is rare,
Made from willow and pear...

They sat for a few moments in silence.

'So,' said David. 'It's round.'

'Could it be in the amphitheatre?' asked Edryn.

'We didn't see anything there made of willow and pear wood,' said Mariad.

'We looked everywhere,' added Tara.

'Round. Could it be a wreath?' asked David. 'Like on the heads of their emperors?'

'It's made for a warrior's hand, not head,' said his twin.

'A dagger?' suggested Edryn.

'That's not round,' said Mariad, 'or made of wood.'

'So it can't be a spear, one of those *pilum* things?' wondered David. 'Not a javelin...'

'Shields are round...' murmured Tara.

'A Roman shield?' Mariad looked puzzled. 'They're made of metal.'

David shook his head. 'Oh, this is more difficult than I thought.'

As his twin held her bag to her heart and felt the Mirror inside, came a whisper:

A circle that's strong...
Found in a lair...

'An animal has a lair – like a wolf,' said Edryn.

Shaking her head, Tara said, 'It doesn't seem to fit.'

Mariad started pacing around the atrium.

'Before we left, the Seer said that the talisman is inside the fortress.'

Simone frowned. 'She could be wrong.'

'She's **never** wrong,' cried Mariad.

'But—' The girl from Rome stopped. Mariad was glowering at her.

David reached for some more grapes. 'So – where in the fortress? One of the barracks?'

As they discussed all the different places, Tara took the Bronze Mirror out of her bag. Moving her hand around it three times, she gazed into it. Grey-white swirls. No whispers came.

'We're going to have to work this out on our own,' said Tara.

Simone cleared her throat. 'Er – I may know something. If I do know, er, where it is – the talisman. If it is there – will you forgive me everything I've done?' She paused. 'Or – haven't done?'

They stared at her.

'Spill the beans, cuz,' said David.

'Beans?'

'Just tell us.'

'*Alora!* Remember, I pardoned you—'

'Simone, speak.' said Tara. 'Now!'

Taking a deep breath, she began, 'There's a vault underneath the governor's room, down a flight of steep stone steps.'

'His lair,' murmured David.

'You go down the steps and along a passage is a strong room. All the important documents of the

Legion are kept there. And money and parchments, too.'

'Could the talisman be there?' asked Edryn.

Simone shrugged. 'I don't know. Down the other passage there's another room; the standard of the Legion with lots of weapons are there.' She shivered. 'It might be there—'

'But that's in the middle of the fortress,' gulped Edryn.

'We'll just have to work out how to get in and out without being caught,' said Tara.

'Why were you in the vault, Simone?' Mariad gave her a fierce look.

'He – the governor – he wanted me – as the – er – assistant priestess – to say some prayers – at the shrine.'

'What prayers?' said David.

'What shrine?' asked Tara.

'What god?' demanded Mariad.

Simone bit her lip.

'It's time to tell the truth, cuz,' said Tara.

Moving the bowls of olives and grapes around the table, Simone hesitated, then muttered, 'Mars, God of War.'

'Simone!' cried Mariad.

'Why did you do that, cuz?'

The young girl blinked several times. 'The governor – he said, it was to make sure the Legion would be successful when – er – when they attack the tribe.'

Mariad went rigid. 'You – you prayed for the Silures to be killed? The tribe? The people who gave you food, gave you shelter?'

Shocked, she turned to face the twins.

'Your cousin has offended our gods, our goddesses. We are lost! The talisman will never be found. The tribe will be slaughtered! The children will all die...'

Simone rocked from side to side, groaning. '*No!* I didn't pray to Mars. I swear I didn't. I don't want bloodshed.' She looked stricken. 'I was so afraid. I prayed to **our** goddess to help me – to help us. To protect us – and the tribe – from the Romans. Believe me,' she pleaded. 'I couldn't think of anything else to do. I had to go with the soldiers. I had to go down to the shrine room. I had no choice.'

'You could've found a way...' muttered Mariad.

Edryn thought for a moment. 'At least you buried the nail – that will protect the tribe from the soldiers.'

Simone stuttered. 'Er – that is – If it **is** in the vault, we'll never find it. There are too many things in there – weapons – er – and there are other passages, too. Soldiers, guards and slaves are around all the time. And the governor. It's – *impossible!*

Mariad threw up her hands. 'No! It isn't! The tribe is depending on us.' She turned her anger towards Tara. 'Why were you sent to us? To help. Help! You've made things worse!'

She hissed at David. 'You – you get arrested and thrown in the dungeons. And Edryn with you.' She swivelled around. 'And you, Simone, descendant of Cleopatra! You followed their orders – why? Then you pray to their warrior god! For their success! Why?'

The granddaughter of the Seer glared at the three time-travellers. 'Is this a game to you? Or are you all trait—'

Edryn ran to her and put his hand over her mouth. 'Stop! You mustn't say it. You mustn't. Once it is said, you cannot take it back – don't say it, Mariad.'

Tara went over to Mariad and touched her arm. Speaking softly, she said, 'You're right to be angry, Mariad. We were sent here to help the tribe – and we will. We made a promise.'

'Yes,' said David. 'We will find the talisman.'

But, Twin, he sent her a mind-message. *What are we looking for?*

We'll know it when we see it... First, we need to get into that vault.

Tara frowned at Simone. 'You will help with every single part of the plan. No running off. Agreed?'

The girl from Rome stared into the flames of the sacred fire. '*Si.* Yes. I agree.'

Stepping back, Mariad looked at her sulky face. 'Simone – is there anything else you'd like to tell us? I feel there is.'

Oh no! I can't tell them I threw the nail into the river...

Sounds of footsteps on the steps of the temple. They froze.

Chapter 12

The Third Riddle

Simone draped her veil over her hair and walked to the top of the temple steps.

Below her was a soldier, his helmet glistening in the sun. He bowed.

'Priestess. The governor requests that you come to Headquarters later this afternoon.'

Simone's mind was racing. *Have I been found out? Has the real priestess returned?*

'He would like you to go down to the shrine room again, and say prayers there. And we, the soldiers of the Second Augustan Legion, beg you, most humbly, to plead with the Goddess Diana to protect us in our coming battle with the Silures.'

She almost faltered. 'When – when will this battle take place?'

The soldier looked puzzled. 'Surely the gods

know? Er – tomorrow. Two hours before daybreak. Will it be an auspicious time? That's what the governor wishes to know.'

Simone gazed across to the hillfort. She did not see the seabirds wheel. She did not hear their cries. She saw nothing, heard nothing.

Tomorrow? And the nail is in the river. Perhaps it fell into the mud. Can I find it and bury it by the gate in time?

'I shall return in an hour – Priestess.'

Simone flung herself on the couch and rocked to and fro. '*O! Mi dispiace.* Sorry! Sorry! It's all my fault. A battle! I'm sorry.' She sobbed as the four stared at her.

'Hey. It's OK, cuz,' said David, patting her shoulder. 'We've been talking about what you did. You didn't have a choice – did she, Mariad?'

The girl shrugged her shoulders.

'Later,' he said, 'when the guards come, go down to the governor's shrine room. Say those prayers – like you said today – to our Goddess, and you can look for the talisman while you're there.'

'And then, bring it here –' said Mariad – 'to us.'

Tara gave her cousin a hug. There's no need to cry. It'll work out.'

'Anyway,' said Edryn. 'There can't be a battle. The soldiers can't leave the fortress. We buried the nails at the four gates. The spell will hold them inside.'

He grinned at his friends.

Simone choked as she wiped the tears from her cheeks. 'You don't understand. I've done something terrible.' She twisted the end of the veil. 'You will hate me.'

Oh no! What now? thought Tara.

Aloud, she said, 'We'd never hate you, cuz.'

'Hey, it can't be that bad,' said David.

'But it is!'

Mariad glared at her. 'Ah... You didn't bury the nail, did you, Simone? You didn't say the words. Did you?'

'No,' she whispered.

'Why not?' Mariad snapped.

Simone gulped. 'I was angry. I believed I was a Roman. I – I threw the nail – in the river!'

They all stared at her in disbelief.

David sighed. 'Seriously bad news, cuz.'

Simone couldn't look at their disappointed faces.

'But then I saw the fighting in the arena. They love blood. They love death. Ergh! The smell!' She touched her heart. '*Mi dispiace*. I'm sorry. I've betrayed you all.'

Mariad threw Simone a look of utter fury.

Edryn shuffled his feet and stared at the birds on mosaic floor while David picked up some kindling and began snapping twigs in two.

Tara heaved a heavy sigh. *It's down to me to sort this out – again. Why does Simone make everything so much harder?*

'What's done is done,' she said. 'Now we need a new plan.'

David mind-messaged his twin. *I so hope you've got one, because I haven't!*

Tara gave her brother The Look. *If you could help me here, that would be good.*

Their cousin was hunched over, sniffing into her veil, repeating, 'It's all my fault.'

'Stop it, cuz,' said Tara firmly. 'Crying isn't useful.'

'We need to come up with the perfect plan,' said David.

'And one that we all keep to this time,' said Mariad, scowling both at Simone and David.

The twins exchanged looks. This was the granddaughter of the Seer. A warrior; strong, courageous, determined. And fierce.

David began walking around the sacred fire. 'So, what do we know? The soldiers are going to attack the tribe before dawn tomorrow.' He stopped. 'But why now? It's only day one of the Games.'

'And they're celebrating their new emperor,' said Tara.

'I heard the soldiers talking when I was in the dungeons,' said Edryn. 'Their ships were wrecked in a storm off the coast. They were bringing grain, so they've lost their cargo.'

'Ah – so they need food for the legion here,' said David. 'And for their fortresses in the north, too. That's why they are planning to attack the tribe.'

'If we find the talisman quickly,' said Tara, 'that will solve everything.'

'Maybe it's kept here, in this temple,' murmured Simone, 'There are scrolls – they are round.'

'But they aren't made of willow and pear,' said Mariad. 'Or for a warrior's hand. It is **in** the fortress.'

'Just to make sure, let's look everywhere,' said Tara.

The five searched for the precious object in all the rooms. Some twice.

When they returned empty-handed, they sat in a circle around the sacred fire.

'Nothing,' said Mariad. 'I keep telling you, it's in the fortress.'

Simone hung her head in despair. 'What can you do?'

'What can we do?' Mariad shouted at her. 'What can—? This was your one task, girl from Rome. To bury the nail.' She tossed her flaming red hair back from her face and fixed her eyes on Simone. 'The future of the tribe was in your hands. It is in your hands.'

Tara looked around at their faces; angry, disappointed, worried.

'Let's sit here, take a few minutes. We need to ask for help from the Goddess.'

If I close my eyes, I can't see Mariad, thought Simone. *She's scary... If only I hadn't thrown the nail...*

David sighed. *If I hadn't gone into the Baths and dived for the gems...*

Edryn clasped his hands together. *If I hadn't tried to attack the soldier...*

Mariad frowned. *If only Raphael could have found the talisman...*

Tara held the Bronze Mirror to her heart. *Help, O Goddess. This looks hopeless...*

'Let's all breathe... In, one, two...'

Inside the temple there was a stillness.

When they opened their eyes, Tara was staring into the Mirror. Mists swirled, then cleared.

Came the whisper:

Seek that which is rare
Away from the glare,
Flat, light and round;
An image – a hound.
Blue stones there will be
Three, to see.

Now, dare, dare,
To descend the stair,
To enter the lair,
To find the circle of willow and pear:
This talisman filled with magic and mystery.
Brave, fearless warriors you must be.

Simone clapped. *'Oh!* The vault! It is in the vault! There are steps – a stair. It's so dark. It must be there. Underneath the governor's rooms!' She gulped. 'That place – it's terrifying. The eyes of the god – they follow you...'

'So warriors we must be!' said Tara.

'But what is the talisman? What are we looking for?' said Simone.

'The image of a hound, blue stones...' murmured David.

Edryn slapped his knee. 'Round, flat, light. Why didn't I think of it before?'

'What? Tell us!' said David.

Edryn stood up and looked around the circle. Taking a deep breath, he announced, 'The talisman – it's the shield of Caratacus. Rare, precious ... mysterious.'

'But shields are made of metal,' said David.

'This one is made of bark – willow and the wood of the pear tree,' said Edryn. 'I remember my father talking about it.'

'Strong, yet light,' said Mariad. 'Warriors have used them in battle throughout time.'

'They stand up to blades and arrows,' said Edryn. 'Caratacus's shield was tough, light – made for speed.'

'My cousin – she had a shield of wood,' whispered Mariad. 'And the hound, that was his animal spirit – it has to be on it.'

'The design, too – squares, red and white,' added

Edryn. 'We Silures have red for battle.'

Mariad nodded.

'*Non capito.* I don't understand. Why have the Romans got it?' asked Simone.

Taking a deep breath, Edryn said, 'When Caratacus escaped after the last battle, and Queen Cartimandua handed him over to the Romans, they must have taken his shield – as a talisman.'

'As long as they have it, they believe they have power over us,' murmured Mariad,

'Magic powers,' whispered Tara.

'We always believed it was in Rome,' said Edryn.

'But, it's under the governor's room,' said Mariad.

'In the vault, and heavily guarded,' said David.

'All their important weapons are placed around the shrine,' said Simone. 'Like their standard. It could be there.'

David leapt up. 'Let's go now! The sooner we go, the sooner we—'

'You'll be arrested again if they find you there,' said Mariad.

'Twin! Wait! Let's not rush in.'

Festina lente, thought Simone. *Make haste slowly...*

'Let's stop and think. We must plan carefully....'

That afternoon, the centurion was in his quarters, counting coins. He had put them into separate piles on his table and was examining the heads of the various emperors.

He smiled with satisfaction. *Claudius, Nero, Augustus...*

A figure appeared in the doorway.

Glancing up, Linus Paulinus saw a slave standing there.

'What is it?'

'Sir, I work in the hospital, tending to the sick and the wounded.'

He frowned at the young man. Dark hair, olive skin. 'You are from—?'

'Judea.'

'Ah, yes.' His lip curled. 'I was there with our new emperor, Titus. We put down the uprising...'

The slave fixed his eyes on the wall behind the centurion.

'... we destroyed Jerusalem, took all the treasures of the Temple to Rome – along with thousands of slaves...'

The slave from Judea did not move. He made no sound.

'Yes, we took all the gold and silver. Titus will build the most magnificent amphitheatre with it...'

He waved his hand. 'Speak.'

The slave's eyes flickered to the table, to the coins. He blinked and took a step back.

'Yes?'

'Er – it – it's about Gaius Tarquin Livinius; the soldier who drove the chariot into the arena and, er, fell. He's recovering from his injuries in the hospital. He wishes to return to his duties.'

'Does he now?' The centurion sighed. 'Is that a problem?'

The slave cleared his throat. 'There's something that I heard, sir – something he said – when he was in a fever.'

Gossip. This could be useful, thought Linus Paulinus. *Usually it's complaints about the rain, the cold, the rations. But sometimes...*

'Continue...'

Looking straight into the centurion's eyes, he said, 'First, sir, may I ask for my freedom and – to become a citizen of Rome?'

The soldier frowned. 'For you to ask for this – the most valuable thing that can be given to you – a slave – this must be something extraordinary.'

The slave fixed his gaze on the piles of *denarii.*

'It is – precious...'

'If what you have to say is important – I could speak to the governor.'

Julius Frontius was standing in front of his family shrine.

'O Apollo and all the gods,' he murmured. 'Where is peace?' He looked out into the courtyard. 'This place, Isca, it is exile. How Ovid must have suffered when he was banished from Rome by Augustus. But I am not a poet. I'm an engineer. Let me return to Rome. Let me use my skills in our great city.'

He bowed and went out into the garden. Long shadows had fallen across the paths. A few stars had begun to appear in the blue-grey sky.

'How I long to stroll with my wife and daughter in our gardens, to sit quietly, to listen to the songs of the birds. But, until I'm given my orders to leave, I must stay here.'

He walked around the garden, stopping to pick some lavender.

And above this fortress lives a Druid. A Seer. A woman of spells, of magic. Only she escaped from Mona, the island in the north. Only she lived, when all her people were slaughtered.

He clasped his hands behind his back. *And so here in Isca, there is always fear. Our fortress is well defended – ramparts, ditches, turrets. We can see the enemy if they attack. Yet it is the presence of the Seer I feel, always. She watches, she waits. For what?*

He wiped his forehead. *And – the tribe – the Silures. Brave. Fierce. Stubborn. We do not understand their ways; they don't understand ours. We are the victors. But – are we?*

He twisted his ring around and around his finger. *Two ships wrecked, the grain from Egypt lost. We needed it – for the men here and for our bases in the north.*

He turned and went into the atrium.

I've had to give the order to surround the hillfort and take the tribe's grain. Have I made the right decision? The Silures have grain and the legion cannot go hungry. Will the tribe give it freely? Or will they fight? Will we have to take it by force?

He stopped at the shrine. 'O Apollo – Let there be no more bloodshed... I beg you.'

Snuffling sounds came from outside the temple. They all stood completely still.

'Let's hide,' said Tara. 'Quickly!'

Covering her face again with the veil, Simone walked through the atrium to the top of the steps.

Below, a young soldier was using all his strength to hold onto a wild boar; it was struggling to escape.

'*Salve*, Priestess! This is for the sacrifice; the offering to Diana, Goddess of the hunt – for our success tomorrow.'

He pulled on the rope; the boar twisted and grunted.

I really am going to be sick. Simone raised her hand. 'A pig?'

The soldier looked confused. 'The wild boar of the Legion, Priestess. The senior centurion gave instructions. So we'll be protected in the coming battle.'

'*Noli timeo.* Be not afraid,' said Simone. 'The day is not propitious for this sacrifice.'

She gazed over towards the hillfort. A buzzard was soaring high above the tree line, circling; it dived and glided away.

'The stars are not aligned. The Goddess Diana desires oil, not blood.'

'Oil?' The soldier tugged at the rope, pulling the boar back towards him. It wriggled and squealed. 'What shall I do with this beast, Priestess?'

Simone gestured towards the woods. 'Diana, Goddess of the Temple, says, "Let it go free. I will hunt it."'

Surprised, the soldier dropped the rope; the boar squirmed, then hurtled towards the forest.

'Oil? Oil?' He muttered as he made his way back towards the barracks.

Simone watched him until he had disappeared then she turned back into the temple.

'Awesome!' said David. 'Great acting!'

She put some kindling on the sacred fire. 'I just hope he doesn't tell the centurion. Pig meat! Ugh!'

Throwing her arms wide, she declared, 'I'm pardoning everything today.'

Mariad was about to speak when Tara said, 'Can we go over the plan once more, before the soldiers come?'

The sound of hurried footsteps came from outside.

'No time! They're here,' whispered Edryn.

They scattered to hide behind screens and doors. A tall young man burst into the atrium.

'Raphael!' cried Mariad.

'The talisman! I've found it for you. Here. I saw it on the centurion's table.' He held out his hand. 'You said it was in a lair. This was in the lair of Linus Paulinus.' Looking around at the surprised faces, he said, 'He was in the Temple in Jerusulem – when it was destroyed.'

David mind-messaged his sister. *Who's this, Twin?*

He's a slave from Judea – a friend of Mariad's. He brought us the tokens to get into the amphitheatre.

They crowded around to look. A gold coin was resting in the palm of his hand.

'Awesome!' said David. 'It's shimmering!'

'The centurion stole it. I was there, hiding in the temple, when the soldiers were stealing our treasures.' He looked at Mariad. 'And you said the talisman was gold.'

Oh, thought Tara. *We didn't say that. He didn't hear all the words of the riddle ...*

'You took it?' Mariad was shocked.

'To help you – and the tribe.'

He smiled around at everyone.

Mariad touched his arm. 'I'm sorry, Raphael. This isn't the talisman we're seeking. We're looking for – a shield, round, made of wood, willow and pear...'

'And we think it's in the vault – below the governor's room.'

Raphael was crestfallen. 'I was so sure—'

Twin! If the centurion realises he's taken it, they'll kill him.

I know.

'Raphael. You must take this back—' began Tara.

Voices could be heard from outside the temple.

'The soldiers have arrived,' said Mariad. 'We have to go.'

Tara slipped the bag with the Bronze Mirror under her robe.

'Do we look the part?'

David and Edryn nodded. 'Cool!'

The sun was setting behind the hills; a band of crimson, orange and dark purple light. An owl screeched as Raphael walked down the temple steps deep in thought, the gold medallion in his hand.

Precious treasure, sacred treasure from the temple, from Jerusalem. But now it could bring about my death.

The boys stayed and waited by the sacred fire. Then, in the grey darkness of twilight, they crept between the columns, skirted around the fortress, and made for the East Gate.

Tarquin steadied himself, pulled a tunic on over his head and fell back down on the stretcher. He examined his sandals. Some of the straps had been ripped off when he'd fallen from the chariot.

I'll have to go to the workshop and tell Vincus – Cassius – someone – to repair these.

He tried to put on his armour, but his shoulder was aching and he couldn't get the breast plate in the right place. *Where's that slave gone? One of my men will have to tighten these leather straps for me.* He shook his head. *I feel strange. Everything keeps moving. There's two of everything.* He sighed. *I must find that boy, Davidus, and teach him a lesson. Whip him, like a horse... Horse... He frightened the horses – that's why I fell. It was all his fault.*

He limped off towards the barracks.

Up in the hillfort, Bethan was dreaming of eel pies. She woke with a start.

Where's my friend? She stretched and looked around.

Children were playing chase in and out of the roundhouses. Aled the blacksmith was at the forge. Bryn was with the horses, checking the harnesses.

Some of the tribe were sharpening swords, others were decorating their arms.

No one will notice if I leave now...

She began to move towards the woods.

'Sit!' The voice came from under the rowan tree.

Bethan sat. After a few minutes, she got up and started again, one paw then another. She sniffed.

'Throw her a bone, Bronwyn,' said the Seer.

Something large and grisly arrived with a thump in front of her.

Maybe I'll stay a while longer.

Bryn walked across to his brother. 'Where are Mariad, Edryn, and those that came from Llanmelin?'

'They were told to find something.' The blacksmith bent over the anvil. 'They're off looking for it.'

Bethan trotted over to the Seer with the bone

and lay down beside her.

When will my friends be back? I miss them.

The Seer looked into her eyes.

It won't be long now.

The spaniel snapped at some flies, chewed some more gristle, settled down and dreamt of rabbits.

The embers of the fire glowed; the full moon was rising.

Flavius was peering through a hole in the stockade fence.

'Hey! We need to escape before the battle starts.'

'Battle?'

'Come here and look! They're painting their arms.'

'What with?

'Woad.'

'Is it all about to happen?' asked Calvus.

'They must be getting ready to attack the fortress,' whispered Flavius. 'And we don't want to be here when it does.'

'We're hostages,' said Magnus. 'They won't harm us. We're more valuable alive. They'll use us to trade with the other tribes.'

Flavius glared. 'Things happen in battle. And I intend to live a long life.'

He turned to look through the hole again and saw their guards moving off.

They were making for a pile of spears, swords and shields near the forge.

Flavius sat back on his heels. *I wonder what—*

Sounds of scratching. An arm came over the gate. A push. The gate had been opened. There was a gap wide enough to squeeze through.

'What—?'

'Let's go!'

Flavius grabbed Magnus's arm. 'See that clump of trees over there? Run!'

Chapter 13

Escape!

It was twilight when three figures entered the fortress, accompanied by two soldiers.

Arriving at Headquarters, the governor came to greet them. 'Three priestesses! What a great honour! Come. Follow me down to the shrine room. You may say the prayers to Mars, the God of War, there.'

A choking noise was quickly muffled.

Came a whisper.

Descend the stairs,
Into the lair...

The trapdoor was already open. Taking a torch, a guard led the way down the steps, along the passage to the vault. Shadows danced over the stone walls.

'Here we stand before Mars, God of War, to offer prayers for the safety of the Legion.' Julius Frontius smiled. 'Come, soldier, light the torch there for the priestesses and we will leave them.'

Silence.

Simone felt her stomach churning as she stared up at the statue.

'Oh! See – there are his horses – they're called Phobos and Deminia; Fear and Terror.'

'I don't care what they're called,' snapped Mariad. 'We need to search for the talisman.'

'*O Dio mio!* His eyes are following me. I'm frightened!'

'So – don't look! You have two choices. Let fear and terror control you – or – choose bravery.'

'Courage, cuz.'

Simone gulped. The flame flickered over the weapons in front of the altar: axes, shields, spears, swords.

'They're all made of metal,' said Tara. 'And those shields are rectangular.'

'The talisman could be in the strong room,' said Mariad.

'I don't think – *Oh no!*' Simone felt panic rising. '*Oh no!* I can't breathe.'

She leant against a wall. 'I need to go up – into the air.'

'You will stay and search with us,' said Mariad.

'This place...' Simone stared at the statue. 'His eyes are following me... I'm afraid. I can't – I—'

We're so close to finding the talisman, thought Tara. Putting her arm around her cousin, she said, 'Remember, breathe in, count to three, hold, then—'

'There's no time for all that,' hissed Mariad. 'We must act. Now. We must return with the talisman – or—'

'Give her a minute... Keep your head down, cuz.'

'Oh, you two wait here. I'll go to the strong room.' Snatching the torch, the girl hurried along the passage.

'The shield isn't there,' whispered Simone. 'They keep the money there, to pay the soldiers. It must be here—'

Minutes later, Mariad appeared with rolls of papyrus and a handful of coins.

She held out a *denarius*. 'Look! Coins – flat and round. This one has a goat on it. This could be the talisman.'

Tara was astonished. 'But Mariad – they're silver... not bark. They are not made of willow and pear.'

'Argh! What was I thinking?' Mariad threw the coins on the floor. She glared at the statue. 'Their god is protecting it.'

There's too much anger here. Help us, Goddess.

'Let's look again,' said Tara. 'It has to be here.'

Mariad glanced around. 'Nothing! It's not here! Oh, this is hopeless!'

Simone shook her head in despair. 'We're never

going to find it...'

'Stop. Think positive thoughts,' said Tara as she took the Mirror out of her bag and held it up. 'It is here. It has to be.'

All around the vault, beams from the Mirror cast rainbows onto the walls, the ceiling, the floor.

Came the whisper:

I, Goddess of the Rainbow,
Banish this darkness, this evil here.
Mars – Your power dissolves.
No more blood will there be; no more fear.

Golden rays shone from the Bronze Mirror directly onto the statue of Mars.

The god's eyes blazed, blood-red, crimson, flame-orange; they flared, burnt, smouldered and – died.

Came the whisper:

Light over darkness always wins.
As the Mirror moves once more, it will bring...

A beam swept over the weapons. A glint. A sparkle.

Below the altar was a shape, half hidden by the metal shields.

'There! Look! There!' whispered Tara. 'Can you see it? Under that red shield?'

'The one with the letters on it?' said Simone. 'LED II AVG.'

Simone lifted up the Roman shield.

Mariad leaned forward. 'I can see red and white... And it's bark!'

Entranced, the three girls stood gazing at the

object. Here was the precious talisman they'd been searching for – Caratacus's shield!

They smiled at each other and clasped hands.

Tara slid the bark shield from under the metal shield and passed it to Mariad.

Holding it, the girl was awestruck. 'This shield he took with him into every battle...'

'Three blue stones and—' whispered Tara.

'A hound.' Simone trembled.

Thank you, O Goddess. Tara let out a deep sigh; the light from the Bronze Mirror dimmed and faded.

'Now we need to smuggle it out,' said Mariad.

'With the governor above us,' said Simone.

They gazed around the vault. Was there anything there that would disguise it?

'We could hide it behind another shield?'

'A priestess holding a Roman shield?'

'We could say it's for an offering?'

'That has to work.' Tara looked at them. 'Otherwise, we're trapped down here.'

The sound of heavy boots came from overhead.

'Sir!'

'Centurion!'

'The legion requests your presence, sir. To give

them courage for the battle ahead.'

'It's not a battle. They'll surround the hillfort and take their grain.' The governor sighed.

'Order the legion to the amphitheatre. I'll address them in the stadium. It's quicker. I've much work to do.'

The girls crouched at the bottom of the steps, listening to their plans.

'Wasn't a boar sacrificed at the Temple of Diana, for the protection of the Legion?' said Julius Frontius. 'You'd think that was enough. Maybe a bull, too?'

Linus Paulinus cleared his throat. 'Sir. About that. Something of interest. The priestess told a soldier earlier that the Goddess Diana didn't require that sacrifice...'

As the two men walked away, their voices became fainter. 'Oil?'

'*Oh No!* They'll think that strange.'

'If the governor's suspicious about the offering,' said Tara, 'he'll realise we're imposters, arrest us and—'

'Punish us severely.'

Simone felt her throat tighten.

'Quick,' said Tara. 'Find something to cover the shield.'

Dusk was turning into night as the boys raced towards the East Gate.

'You there! Halt!'

'Head down. Run.' David rushed on and hid behind a timber post near the entrance.

Where's Edryn?

A small figure hurtled past; he reached out and gripped a shoulder.

'David! It's you!'

'We'll slip past the guards, hide near the barracks, and wait for the girls to arrive.'

'It'll soon be midnight,' said Edryn. 'We must get back to the hillfort.'

'But we haven't got the talisman yet.'

'Shush! Soldiers!'

The boys squashed themselves against the wall as two soldiers strode by.

'So we're off to the amphitheatre – again.'

'Just as I was sharpening my *gladius*.'

The legionaries disappeared into the gloom.

David heaved a sigh. 'Cool. The barracks will be empty.'

As he moved towards the gate, Edryn muttered, 'Wait! The guard's changing.'

'*Salve!* Password?'

'Remus.'

'Hey, Crispus! That was loud. What if a spy was nearby?'

'All the spies have left! They're in the hillfort now!'

'Anyone seen Tarquin?'

'Last I heard, he was in the hospital, raving about taking revenge on his deadly enemy.'

'And where is he? That Davidus?'

'Who knows? Interesting kind of fighting, that.'

'Give me the usual cut and thrust.'

'Trident and net is my favourite! Now, when I was in Gaul...'

David's leg started to cramp. *Why don't they go?*

Simone crept up the stone steps and peered around the governor's room.

'No one's here,' she called.

'Look for something to cover the shield,' whispered Tara.

At that moment, the fluttering of something long and white caught Simone's eye. A large woman, dressed in a robe, was waddling across the courtyard.

'Come up here now,' said Simone. 'Quick! We have to hide!'

The girls slid behind the wooden screen.

'I need to speak to the governor. Now!' a voice demanded.

'He's in the amphitheatre, Priestess.'

'Escort me there this instant! I hear there are

imposters, dressed as priestesses, performing strange rituals, refusing to sacrifice a wild boar. I go to Burrium for a few days to buy Samian-ware, the very best bowls for the Temple, then —'

'Do you wish to wait here, Priestess?'

'Wait? No! In fact, I need to attend to the sacred fire. I must make sure it's still burning. You may escort me to the temple.'

'But the governor ordered me to stay here—'

'Now!'

Hushed voices carried on the cool night air as two soldiers slipped out of the East Gate. The boys shrank further back into the shadows.

'How much have you got in your arm purse?'

There was a clinking of coins.

'My pay for six months. You?'

'Four months. I lost ten *denarii* playing dice with Flavius.'

'Everyone loses against him! I swear by all the gods he cheats!'

'Remember where we bury this.'

'As if we'd forget!'

'Will the tide be out?'

David put his head around the wooden post. *They're going towards the river.*

214

A mind-message came from Tara: *Twin! Where are you?*

By the East Gate. We'll be at the barracks soon. Hurry! Have you found the talisman yet?

An owl flew out of an oak, swept in front of the governor and his centurion, and disappeared into the twilight.

Startled for a moment, they continued walking back from the amphitheatre.

'That's the plan. Two hours before dawn. Take three cohorts, march up through the woods to the hillfort, surround it and surprise the Silures.'

'Yes, sir. Three cohorts. Battle-hardened men, all. Their warriors have no discipline. Unlike us...'

'Yet they have passion. Remember that. They're defending their land. Subdue them quickly. And with no, or little, bloodshed. And –' he lowered his voice as they entered the South Gate – 'remember my orders – do not touch the Seer. Not under any circumstances. Disaster would befall us—'

Walking along the via principalis, they passed a barracks and officers' houses.

'You believe in her power, sir?'

'We can't take any chances.'

The centurion nodded. 'But we have their talisman, sir.'

'We do.'

'With its magical powers. As long as we have it, we cannot be defeated.'

The governor was silent.

'It's well hidden in the vault, sir. Guarded by Mars, our god of war.'

'Then, Linus Paulinus, success will be ours.'

In the governor's atrium, two slaves were filling up bowls with fruit and nuts.

The three girls crouched behind the screen, not daring to move.

'The governor will be back soon. We need a distraction,' whispered Tara.

Mariad pointed to a tall pot with two handles, standing just inside the entrance to the courtyard. 'What's that?'

'An amphora,' said Simone. 'It's full of oil.'

'Perfect!' Stretching out her leg, Mariad pushed it with her foot.

Crash!

Fragments of pottery scattered; oil began oozing, trickling, then flowing all over the mosaic floor.

'Sounds like something's broken,' called a slave.

They rushed out into the courtyard. Every crevice was filling up with yellow liquid.

'Ah! It's slippery!

'My ankle!'

'Clean this up before the governor returns, or we'll both be flogged.'

The girls tiptoed out from behind the screen and hurried through the atrium.

At the entrance, they looked left and right. Two figures, deep in conversation, were coming towards them.

'Run! Opposite direction!'

Racing down the main street, they stopped for a moment, resting against a wall where the deep shadows hid them.

After catching their breath, they stood straight; priestesses once more.

'And now we walk slowly,' said Tara.

'Alora! Which way?'

'East.'

Inside the barracks, the boys were examining the armour. Edryn held up a breastplate. 'Does this go over our tunics?'

David thought back to films he'd seen: *Ben Hur*, *Gladiator*. 'Ye-es. I think this shoulder thing goes on first, then these metal strips.'

'It's heavy.'

After adjusting Edryn's armour and fastening the leather ties, David checked his friend's belt.

'Sword on the right. Dagger on the left. Or is it the other way around?' David stepped back. 'There. You'll definitely pass for a Roman soldier.'

They grinned at each other.

'Now help me on with all this gear.'

'What about boots?' asked Edryn, holding up a pair.

'Too big. Let's wear our sandals.'

A door banged. The boys jumped.

Three figures fell in through the door.

'Cool! You made it!'

'Did you find the talisman?' asked Edryn.

Simone adjusted the red cloak she was wearing over her robe. '*Oh!*' she gasped. 'It was so difficult—'

'To get out –' said Tara – 'without being seen.'

'Even if we'd found it—' said Mariad.

David was shocked. 'You didn't find it?'

Flinging off the cloak with a flourish, Simone revealed – a metal shield.

'That's Roman,' said Edryn, disappointed.

Simone turned it over so the boys could see behind the metal was—

'Caratacus's shield!'

'What a brilliant place to hide it,' said David.

'We must go, before they realise we've taken it

back,' said Mariad.

Throwing off their robes, the girls pulled the body armour on over their tunics.

'Don't forget the shoulder plates,' said David. 'You need to lace the leather bits through the shirt thing.'

Simone wriggled.

'Now helmets.'

'Do we need to wear one with a crest and plumes?' asked Simone.

'Only centurions wear those,' said David. 'But, being the leader, maybe I should...'

Several minutes later, the five stood staring at each other.

'We look just like Roman soldiers.'

'Grab a shield. Now this is what we do next—' began David.

Tarquin had searched all over the fort for his enemy. His head still hurt; he shook it from side to side. The buzzing in his ears wouldn't stop.

When I find him, I will... Oh, I don't feel good. There's the barracks. I'll go in there for a while. Sit on my bed...

As he stumbled through the door, he stopped and stared. At the other end of the long corridor, he

saw a Roman soldier. A helmet. The centurion? No
– no crest, but the eyes looked familiar.

Am I dreaming this? He tried to focus. Four other
shapes came into view; more soldiers.

One turned and looked at him. Dark brown eyes.
The priestess? Shaking his head, he stared again.
The figures had vanished.

*That blow to my head must have been worse
than I thought. Were they real? Are they ghosts?
Should I follow them?*

Five soldiers marched towards the East Gate.
Simone gripped the handle of Caratacus's shield so
tightly her knuckles ached.

Shortly before the gate, they stopped and leant
against the stone wall.

'I'll go in front,' whispered David. 'Then Mariad
and Edryn, Tara and Simone behind. Two by two.
March. Keep moving forward. Don't stop. I'll call
out the password, "Romulus"...'

'It's Remus,' said Edryn.

'Oh, yes, "Remus". Wrong wolf... Then we march
out of the Gate.'

They nodded.

'When we are halfway across the field, we'll form
a *testudo*.'

'A what?'

'Like a tortoise. We'll lock our shields together, keep our heads down, and go forwards. Make for the woods. Stop for nothing, for nobody.'

'Remember,' said Mariad, 'we're warriors.'

'And we have the talisman,' said Edryn. 'We—'

Tara frowned. 'Shush.'

At the East Gate, the guards were discussing the coming battle. 'Three cohorts only will be going to attack the tribe, then?'

One glanced idly at the group. 'Password!'

'Remus,' shouted David in a deep voice.

As they strode through the gate, they heard a familiar voice.

'Stop! Stop them! The priestess is there! And Davidus. Thief!'

'Keep marching,' muttered David. 'In a few seconds, form the *testudo*; move forwards quickly.'

The guards stood in front of the young soldier, who was swaying on his feet.

'If it isn't Gaius Tarquin Livinius!'

'What's your problem?'

'Too much wine?'

'Too many blows to the head!'

Tarquin grabbed the soldier's arm.

'Davidus – and the priestess – she isn't a priestess... I don't know who she is... She wouldn't take my curse... They're escaping... They must've stolen something... He's a traitor and a spy... She's a spy...'

'Oh, lots of spies!'

Two guards crossed their spears to stop him going further.

'You've had a bad accident—'

'– in the amphitheatre.'

'You hit your head.'

'Go back to the hospital.'

'Take some more of those potions...'

Tarquin stamped his foot. 'I tell you – they're escaping. She – the priestess – not the priestess – she let the offering for the sacrifice go – the wild boar escaped. I – I heard. They are the enemy!'

'You're seeing things! Those are our soldiers, practising drills for the battle ahead.'

'A battle you won't be in!'

Out of the shadows came a tall, broad-shouldered soldier.

'Sir!' The guards stood to attention and saluted.

'Ah!' The centurion glared. 'So here's the bravest soldier in the Second Augustan Legion!'

Tarquin squinted at the figure. He swayed as he tried to stand to attention.

'Er – Gaius Tarquin Livinius, sir.'

'You left the hospital without permission. Your cohort has been searching for you.'

'I – er – I—'

'A serious complaint has been made about you.'

The young soldier looked puzzled. 'A complaint?'

'At the Games. You stole a chariot and damaged it. The horses were injured, too. Valuable horses.'

'No – I had to take it – er – borrow it, because...'

He broke off and pointed to the *testudo.*

'There – there – look! He's getting away again. Davidus. And that Eddidus. They're escaping.'

By the light of the moon, the *testudo* could be seen in the meadow.

'Practising drills, sir,'

'He's not right in the head, sir.'

'Take him to headquarters,' said Linus Paulinus. 'The governor's waiting.'

Tarquin was horrified. 'No! I'll pay for the chariot and the horses... I have my pay—'

The centurion glared. 'This isn't about the chariot. Your secret has been revealed, Gaius Tarquin Livinius. You have destroyed *Pax Romana*, the Peace of Rome, all on your own – here – at Isca. For that, you will be punished. Harshly.'

'What? I didn't – I couldn't – I...' babbled the young soldier.

The centurion fixed him with a grim stare. 'Some weeks ago, you killed a child, a young girl, up there at the hillfort. A Silures.'

Tarquin swallowed hard.

'You spoke of this in your fever,' said Linus Paulinus. 'The governor is angry! Livid! After twenty-five years of war with this tribe, he believed there was a chance for peace. But, when the body of that small child was found, stabbed, the Silures began to prepare for war.'

'She was only a—'

'Silence! Your first punishment is you will stand before the Legion. Your belt will be taken from you.'

'No!'

'And for your second punishment – the new governor, Julius Agricola, intends to fight the Ordovices. The gold and silver mines must be protected. You will join his men.'

'No! I beg you—'

'Think yourself fortunate. For the next two decades, you will be defending the Empire in the northern reaches of this island!'

Tarquin's head was spinning. 'No! Not the north – ice – snow... I never meant—'

'Take him away!'

The five had marched across to the edge of the woods.

Simone was in the middle, locked into the *testudo.* Her fingers ached.

I must keep hold of this.

'Keep together. Forward.'

They moved towards the trees.

'How much further?

'Another minute...'

From the East Gate came a shout.

'Soldiers! Back to barracks! Drills are over.'

The *testudo* halted.

'Make him believe we're returning. Begin to wheel around. Slowly,' said David. 'Then, when I shout "Run", dash for the woods.'

'Simone. Run like a hare, up the track to the hillfort,' said Tara. 'Give the shield to the Seer. Don't stop! Everyone's counting on you.'

'Don't let us down this time,' hissed Mariad.

They had half wheeled towards the fortress when a call came from the East Gate.

'Soldiers! Return!'

The *testudo* stopped; they unlocked their shields.

'Go, Simone! Go!'

Using the side of the metal shield, she pushed aside brambles, leaping over branches and trailing ivy. Her heart was bursting. *Andiamo!* Let's go!

She climbed higher and higher. The path became steeper. *Nothing, no one, must stop me now.*

Moths swirled around her head. Glancing up at the night sky, she shivered. A bat flew across the moon and hung there for a moment. Several bats swirled around her. She felt their breath on her cheeks.

'Argh!'

Through the briars, she forced her way forward until—

'Flavius!'

Standing in the middle of the track was the young soldier. Behind him were the hostages.

'What are you doing here?' he demanded.

Simone was rigid. *Let me keep this precious shield safe, O Goddess.* Hoping her voice would carry, she called out, 'Flavius! Excellent! You've escaped!'

His eyes narrowed. 'Where are you going?'

She pretended to be breathless. 'Orders. I – I was spying on the Silures, found out their plans – when they're going to attack – Isca. So I – I slipped away and reported this news to – to the governor.'

She could hear rustling in the undergrowth. *Please let the others hear me.*

'Why are you wearing armour?' asked Flavius, frowning . 'And holding a *scutum?*

A what? Ah, a shield.

'The governor told me what to do.' She held her side and grimaced.

'Stand halfway up the hill in these woods, and look like a Roman soldier, he said. I – I must go higher up and stay there. Wait until the cohorts arrive.'

The soldiers exchanged puzzled glances.

'Sounds strange,' said Flavius.

She shrugged. 'It was a trick he used when he was in Gaul.'

At that point, an animal bounded down the track, stopped, sniffed Simone's feet, and wagged her tail.

'No, Bethan!' she muttered.

Calvus aimed a kick at the puppy. 'Get away, beast!'

The spaniel yelped, growled, and began barking. *I will nip his heels.*

'Stop biting my ankle!'

Bethan backed away and continued barking.

'The tribe will hear this and we'll be captured again,' said Magnus.

'Let's just get back to the fortress,' said Flavius. He gave Simone a curious look. 'Shall I mention this to the governor?'

She nodded. 'Yes. Say I'm carrying out his orders – to the letter.'

He followed the others as they hurtled down the track and reached the edge of the woods.

'What are all these weapons doing here?' said Magnus.

'I don't care!' cried Flavius. 'Let's get to the Baths, scrape off the dirt of that place, and eat some good food.'

Racing across the field, they arrived at the South Gate.

'Password?'

Chapter 14

The Eclipse

Julius Frontius leant over to smell the lavender, then he dipped his fingers in the bubbles of the fountain.

Soon it will be time for the cohorts to leave the fortress, he thought.

Someone nearby cleared his throat.

'Centurion.'

'Sir. Has the standard-bearer been down to the vault?'

The governor waved his hand. 'Possibly.'

'With your permission, sir. I'll check.'

Taking a torch, the centurion went down the flight of steps. As he reached the bottom, he saw rolls of papyrus scattered all over the floor.

'Who's here?'

He went along the passage to the strong room and stopped. The lid of the metal box was wide open.

'What in the name of Mars has happened here?'

Silver coins lay strewn all around, mixed in with the Legion's records.

'Show yourself!'

Silence.

Hurrying to the vault, he saw the shields beneath the shrine had been moved.

Round ones were leaning against one side of the altar, rectangular shields over on the other.

Who's done this?

Thrusting the torch into every corner of the vault, he searched for the talisman.

By Mars! Where's the shield! It must be here!

Linus Paulinus felt his heart racing. With total desperation, he ran down every passage, into every room, nook and cranny. He looked, again and again. There was no sign of it. The talisman had vanished.

He walked up the steps in a daze.

'Centurion. You look troubled.'

'Sir. Someone's been in the vault. Your scribe, perhaps?'

'No, he's coming later. The three priestesses were down there. To say prayers at the shrine.'

The centurion looked stricken.

'Then perhaps an animal—'

'Speak.'

'The talisman – the shield of Caratacus. It's vanished.'

Julius Frontius stared in disbelief at the soldier. 'Have you searched everywhere?'

'Yes, sir. Twice, three times.'

The governor followed the centurion down to the vault. It was true. Someone had taken the talisman.

She looked like my daughter. Yet she was a thief...

'This is a bad omen, sir.'

'Say nothing of this to anyone. No one must know.'

The centurion hesitated. 'Sir. There's more news. Flavius and his men have escaped from the hillfort.'

'Good.'

'They met your spy in the woods.'

Puzzled, the governor turned to face him. 'My spy? I have no spy.'

'A young girl. She'd brought them food when they were prisoners, a day or so ago. Tall, olive skin, dark hair. She said she was from Rome.'

'Did she?' The governor selected a fig, examined it, and put it back in the bowl. 'Interesting.'

'She was wearing armour and carrying a *scutum*. She told Flavius she was a spy... Your spy.'

Julius Frontius sighed. 'And a priestess.'

'Was she your spy, sir? You might have told me—'

'No. She was a fraud, an imposter.' He grimaced.

'And a good one.'

The centurion frowned. 'Should we—?'

'There's nothing we can do about it.'

'Do you think she stole the talisman, sir?'

'I think she probably did.'

'A traitor!'

The governor fixed the soldier with a hard stare. 'Let us not forget, Centurion. One of our legionaries killed their child. A child!'

The soldier looked blank. 'The legion needs grain, sir.'

'Then go. Bring back the grain. But remember my orders. Do not touch the Seer.'

It was close to midnight. The moon was full. A nightingale was singing from the tallest silver birch in the glade.

Around the fire, the tribe was listening to Bryn.

'Now the hostages have escaped, we need to attack the fortress – tonight.'

He stopped. Simone burst into the clearing, holding out a metal shield.

'We – we found it,' she panted. 'Must take to – the Seer—'

Bryn strode across to her. 'Why have you brought us this? A Roman shield!'

Simone had not expected that. 'No! You don't understand. Look!'

Turning over the Roman shield, she took out the bark shield. 'See! Here's the talisman!'

Startled, Aled cried, 'The shield of Caratacus!'

Bryn sneered. 'What? No! It can't be. That shield's in Rome.'

At that moment, Mariad and Edryn arrived, with the twins and Bethan close behind.

'Isn't it wondrous?' shouted Edryn. 'It was in the vault! We—'

Bryn stood back, his arms folded. 'How do we know this is Caratacus's shield?'

Aled pointed out the emblems. 'It has to be, brother. Look – the hound, the three blue stones, the design – red and white squares, spirals on the handle.'

The blacksmith held it up high. 'Look on this, Silures! The shield of Caratacus! Against the Roman invaders he led us!'

The whole tribe, men, women and children, their faces rapt, gazed at the talisman in awe.

'I remember him in battle – a great warrior he was,' nodded an old man. 'That is his shield.'

'Edryn. Proud of you, I am,' said Aled, clapping his son on his shoulder. 'Sit. Tell us the story of your search.'

'Granddaughter of the Seer,' called a woman. 'Grateful to you, we are!'

'We honour you all,' said Aled, smiling at Simone

and the twins. 'You will have faced many perils. Our thanks to you, always, and forever.'

'Now we must take it to the Seer,' said Tara.

'She's in the sacred grove.' Aled started to give the shield to Mariad.

The girl shook her head. 'No. Simone must take it to her.'

To the rowan tree they walked. Moonlight shone on the figure sitting alone.

A golden glow surrounded her.

Stepping forward, Simone placed the bark shield in front of her.

The Seer began to chant, wafting sage leaves over the talisman.

The scent drifted on the light breeze.

'Why is she doing that?' whispered Simone.

'The shield must be cleansed,' said Mariad. 'The Romans kept it under the statue of Mars for many years; it was surrounded by dark energy.'

Around the fire, in the clearing, Edryn was telling the story of the search. 'Then the soldiers were saying they'll attack two hours before dawn...'

In a moment, the quietness of the night was shattered. Bryn leapt up and began waving his sword around, shouting, 'Now we can take revenge! Let's attack the Romans tonight! Burn down their Customs House! Destroy their fortress.'

A young man, an image of a wolf on his arm, jumped up. 'Yes! Let's go!'

Men and women began picking up their weapons.

Aled raised his hand. 'No! This is not the way. Our gods, our goddesses, do not seek revenge—'

'But Edryn has just told us three cohorts will attack us before the sun rises,' cried Bryn. 'We can creep through the woods. Pick them off, one by one. Who's with me?'

Gripping his arm, Aled glared at his brother. 'Stop this. The spirits have spoken. Listen to the Seer. She comes.'

Sitting cross-legged by the fire, the Seer spoke. Of Caratacus, the fearless Leader... Of Boudica, warrior queen of the Iceni; she who stood against the Roman invaders. Of all those who had resisted the Roman Empire.

'Silures. I speak of the past. Our world has changed. We are faced with two choices. To continue along the old path – the path of war, and be crushed. Or to listen to the spirits – choose the way of peace, and live. The time is now. Choose.'

From her leather pouch, the Seer took out a crystal; long, thin, purple.

All waited expectantly.

As she held up the amethyst wand, lights from the fire flickered, catching its spidery threads; red, purple, violet.

Not a sound was uttered.

The Seer closed her eyes. Minutes passed; her face became long, her cheeks hollowed. Swaying back and forth, she murmured: 'The veil of time, it shimmers, it parts... I see... I see... night blackness, the deepest darkness, before our world was created.'

She took a breath. 'I see... I see... below the earth, mountains of fire, rivers of red-black fire. A hollow of rock. This crystal is forming, it brings wisdom, it brings peace. A bridge between our world and the spirits.'

Tara glanced at Simone. Her eyes were fixed on the wand.

'This amethyst crystal is a protector – from wild thoughts; thoughts of anger, violence and revenge.' Her voice grew softer. 'I ask the spirits to cleanse all here. Now Silures! Set your minds for peace. Let your thoughts become as clear as the streams that trickle from the mountains in the north. As pure as the rivers that flow from the hills in the west. Let your minds be filled with light, with love.'

Nothing stirred. No one moved.

The Seer came out of the trance, shuddered, and opened her eyes.

'Silures, I hold the Amethyst Wand. Say your wishes...'

Desidero... I wish... thought Simone.

The Seer smudged the crystal with sage leaves. The ritual had been completed.

She looked over towards her granddaughter.

'Mariad. Speak.'

The girl walked in a circle around the fire, stopped, turned, and gazed around at the tribe.

'Silures. Friends. Poison has infected this tribe. Someone has been keeping a dark secret. A secret that must be revealed now.'

Edryn threw a log onto the fire. It crackled and roared into life as the tribe muttered amongst themselves.

'A question. How did the hostages escape?'

'Sit down, girl,' called Bryn.

Mariad raised her voice. 'I'll tell you.' She paused. 'When my friends and I were in the woods earlier, we overheard the hostages talking. Puzzled, they were. Why had a Silures opened the gate for them?'

Aled shook his head. 'No one here would do that.'

Mariad continued. 'A man's arm, they saw. With a design. An animal.'

She stared at Bryn. 'A snake!'

'Brother! What is this?' cried the blacksmith.

Bryn lowered his head.

'At the quay you were, listening to the news of shipwrecks, the grain that was lost—'

'No! That wasn't me...'

'The Romans had to get more grain,' said Mariad. 'You knew it had to be from the tribe. And it gave you a perfect chance for revenge. You opened the gate, let the hostages escape. Then you used this to persuade the warriors to fight.'

'It wasn't me—'

Tara stood up. 'I saw you – by the Customs House.'

'Brother – we need to hear the truth,' said Aled.

Bryn glared around at them all. 'Yes. I was at the quayside. Yes, I let the hostages go. Why? For revenge – revenge for my daughter. They killed her. So – I must kill them. Peace? I have no peace...!' He choked. 'If Caratacus were here, he would attack.' He put his head in his hands and began sobbing.

The Seer spoke: 'Hide not your pain behind Caratacus. Choose your path now. Let go of your rage, your anger. You are destroying yourself.'

Gazing up to the heavens, she said, 'It is the night of the full moon. I have been told – a sign will appear. Your enemies will be overcome with fear. They will not attack.'

'No!' shouted Bryn. 'I know—'

'Silence! You know nothing! Tonight, our Goddess has spoken: Never again will the Romans attack this tribe.'

Getting to her feet, she grasped her staff. 'Of the line of Druids, I am. On the sacred Isle of Mona I was born. Here was I sent. To show you a new path, a new beginning. It is the time.'

Turning to her granddaughter, she said, 'Mariad, bring the shield.'

To the tribe she said, 'Silures, People of the Rock – come with me to the crag!'

David whispered, 'What's happening, Twin?'

'I don't know.' Tara took the Bronze Mirror from her bag.

Came the whisper:
Go now with the Seer,
Shine the light from the Mirror,
By her remain near,
Have no fear,
There will be such a sight
on this darkest night.

Clouds swept across the full moon as the centurion peered into the dense woodland.

Behind him, the cohorts were lined up in their formations, ready to attack.

Mars, God of War, give me strength for the battle ahead.

Movement in the trees; shadows, shapes, a rustling in the undergrowth.

Chariots? No. The terrain is too rough. A

surprise attack? A quick strike and they'll disappear into the woods.

He heaved a sigh. *We must surround the hillfort. Take their grain. But no bloodshed – the governor's orders. His appetite for war, for conquest, has gone. Mine hasn't.*

He felt for his belt; his *gladius* was there, sharpened that day. *Short stabs. That will do it.* He gazed up at the shimmering moon. *It seems bigger, brighter, red orange. Mars must be with us.*

In the distance, a wolf began to howl.

'When will he give the order?' muttered a soldier.

Time passed. A shadow began to creep over the moon. Within minutes, only a slender curve remained. A soft light; a silvery crescent.

All was plunged into total darkness. Ink-black. Pitch-black. Night-black.

From across the river, a cold breeze blew.

The moon has vanished. Linus Paulinus felt a chill creeping into his bones.

Behind, his men began murmuring.

'Where's the moon gone?'

'Indeed, this is a bad omen.'

The soldiers waited, hardly daring to breathe.

The silence deepened.

High above them came a voice, deep and strong.

'Soldiers of Rome! Know this! Our Goddess is gravely displeased. A child of this tribe has been killed. An innocent child murdered.'

Linus Paulinus sighed heavily.

'Who killed her?' whispered the standard-bearer. 'Not me...'

'O Mars! Is that their Seer?'

'Has **she** stolen the moon?'

'A trick,' the centurion called over his shoulder. 'Stand firm, men.'

A raven croaked.

'These are bad omens.'

'Soldiers of Rome!' The Seer's voice carried to the men below. 'You ask when will you conquer the Silures? The answer is – never! You ask, when will you crush their spirit? Never! You ask, when will they be your slaves? Never!' She paused. 'You fight for an empire that is cruel. You invade our lands – to take our gold, our silver, our lead. You kill our peoples. Why? For the glory of your emperor! Glory is nothing! Power is nothing!'

The centurion hissed, 'Don't listen, men.'

The Seer continued. 'You bring war; you bring bloodshed. Before you came to these shores, we lived in peace with Nature. You have destroyed our ancient forests, built tracks through our sacred places. Men of Rome, our Goddess sees your deeds. Wait and watch. Your actions will be punished.'

Fear began to spread from one cohort to the next.

'Steady, men,' called their leader.

'More powerful than Mars,' declared the Seer. 'More powerful than your warrior god, is our goddess. This very night, she has taken the moon.'

The legionaries stared up at the sky in awe.

The night was pitch-black. There was no moon, yet stars filled the sky.

'Never have I seen this before,' murmured the standard-bearer.

A sudden flash. Beams of light encircled a figure. Above them, high on a rocky ledge, a woman stood.

'The Seer!' murmured the centurion.

'Sir, I could spear her from here—'

'No.'

'Look on this!' called the Seer as rays, purple, indigo, violet, streamed down from her hand onto the men below.

The soldiers craned their necks to see.

'What's she holding?'

'It's long, thin, pointed...'

'I've seen them in Gaul—'

The standard-bearer was astonished. 'A wand – a crystal wand—'

In seconds, purple lights encircled them; a circle of calm held them.

I've never felt like this... Strangely peaceful, thought the centurion.

A young girl stepped forward into the light.

'Who's that?'

'Looks familiar... but – it can't be – she's dead.'

'A ghost!'

Mariad was lifting something high above her head.

'Look on this shield!' called the Seer. 'Round, made of bark. Three stones there are; blue, glittering. See! Red and white squares. See! A hound.'

The standard-bearer muttered, 'Sir. It can't be. It was in the vault.'

Linus Paulinus groaned.

Again, the Seer spoke, 'This is the shield of Caratacus. Whoever has this cannot be conquered. That you know well!'

Shocked murmurings came from the soldiers.

'True, true.'

'Caratacus – he was a fierce warrior.'

'But **we** had the shield...'

'How did she get it?'

'Magic...'

The centurion faced his men. 'Men of the Second Augustan Legion—'

No one was listening to him.

'They'll slaughter us in these woods.'

'We've no chance.'

'They've got the talisman.'

'And a crystal wand...'

'Their Goddess has stolen the moon...'

The Seer's voice carried from the Heavens.

'And now I prophesy:
Before the year's end,
To your cost,
Two of your cities
will be forever lost.

A mountain erupts,
Lava flows to the sea,
Destroying your people

As they flee.

The burning ash
Buries their cries;
Held frozen in time;
So many die.

The Gods take those
Lying as they sleep
Your people will perish,
Your empire will weep.'

The silence was shattered by a scream. A fox?
The soldiers shifted from one foot to the other.
'Sir. We cannot fight against this.'
'Not the power of their Goddess.'
Looking back at the men, the standard-bearer addressed the centurion.
'Sir? Your orders?'
Linus Paulinus looked helplessly at the confused and stricken men.
'We – er – we won't attack now. Perhaps tomorrow or – er – another time—'
At these words, the men broke rank. Stumbling across the field, they fled towards the fortress and a kind of safety.

Julius Frontius gazed up at the stars. A red-tinted glow ringed the full moon.

How extraordinary.

The centurion arrived, breathless.

'Sir. I do not bring good news.' He paused. 'We were about to move up through the woods when the – er – the moon vanished. The night was black. So dark we couldn't see our hands before us. The men believed Mars had abandoned us. They were in fear of the Druid woman – the Seer.'

'Yes,' said the governor. He went inside and examined some scrolls on his desk.

'Sir – she stood above us; floating amongst the trees. A vision. A bright light, like gold, was all around her. She was holding a crystal – a wand... an amethyst wand. That's what the men said. She pointed it straight at us. Purple lights surrounded the cohorts. I – we – they – all – had the strangest feelings—'

Selecting a papyrus, Julius Frontius began studying the design; circles, rectangles, spirals. 'And the talisman?'

'Sir. They have it. A young girl held it aloft. This brilliant light shone upon it. From where it came, I know not. The men were terrified. How could this happen? No moon to give light, yet every colour of the rainbow was beamed onto the shield – yellow, orange, green, blue, red...' Shaking his head, he said. 'It was magic...' Linus Paulinus stuttered. 'I – the men – they fled, sir.'

He stared at the floor, not wanting to admit that he'd joined them.

Glancing up at the soldier, Julius Frontius said, 'Order a messenger up to the hillfort now. Request talks with the tribe at midday. Tell the scribe he will be coming. We'll be making peace.'

'But, sir—'

'*Pax,* Linus Paulinus. Peace.'

At daybreak, the tribe were gathering in the clearing as David was coming out of the roundhouse with Bethan.

He stopped and called to Tara and Simone inside. 'Something's happening. You'd better come quickly.'

Aled was looking around at all those sitting before him. The Seer arrived with Mariad, and sat on a woven seat underneath an oak. She nodded to the blacksmith.

'On this day,' he began, 'when the sun is high, the governor wishes to meet, to discuss peace.'

Bryn shouted. 'No! We have the talisman, we can win!'

'Brother!' Aled sighed. 'That time has gone.'

The twins and Simone sat on the edge of the glade, near a copse of birches, to listen. Bethan jumped into David's lap and nuzzled his neck.

'And I'm glad to see you too,' he whispered. 'Now behave. This is serious.'

The Seer wrapped her cloak around her. 'The Goddess has spoken...'

All waited. There was a long silence.

Shuddering, she began to enter a dream-like state.

'For many years, these invaders will stay. Seasons will come, seasons will go.

From within their Empire, there will be violence – and from without. Wars will be fought. Their enemies will attack. Rome will burn. Their Empire will crumble and fall – as do all empires in time.'

'By then we'll be with our ancestors,' said Bryn.

'Silures. Prepare to leave this hillfort. Go to your tribal place near the wide sea. Go to the hill, to the circle of stones. Live in peace there. Graze your cattle, raise your children in your own ways. Keep your language. Keep your customs. Honour our gods and goddesses.'

She nodded. 'I hear. I will tell them. Silures. Go down to the flat lands, there, cast the shield of the warrior, Caratacus, onto the open waters. An offering of thanks it is, to the Goddess.'

There was a shocked silence. This, the tribe had not expected.

'Go – to Llanmelin!' muttered Bryn.

The Seer continued. 'I see a place there for you – near the big waters. An important place for many a year. The centre for this tribe.'

She shuddered. Her head fell onto her chest.

Twin, where does she mean?

It must be Caerwent.

After several minutes, she opened her eyes.

Aled asked, 'Seer, will you stay with us?'

She shook her head.

'My task here is completed. I will travel west, cross the great water, and there remain.'

Where's she going, Twin?

To Ireland.

Chapter 15

<u>Afon Llwyd</u>

The twins and Simone watched as the tribe prepared to leave the hillfort.

Aled was lifting the anvil onto a cart; Bryn was collecting tools. A couple of weaving looms and spinning wheels were being loaded onto another cart, while children played around the empty stockade.

A cool breeze brushed Tara's cheek. She touched her bag and felt the outline of the Bronze Mirror

Came a whisper:

One thing more before you leave:
Return to The Seer as you must receive...

David was about to whistle for Bethan when a tall, thin young man stumbled into the clearing.

Bryn reached for his sword. 'Who are you?'

'I'm a slave... was.' He panted. 'I've run away.'

'He's a Roman spy!'

Mariad ran over to him. 'No. This is Raphael, my friend.' She looked at Aled. 'Remember? He brought little Alys back the day she got lost in the woods.'

The blacksmith nodded. 'Speak.'

'My name's Raphael. Judea was my country. Now it's a province of Rome. When I was a child, I saw the Romans soldiers killing my family, and thousands of my people. They destroyed our temple in Jerusalem.' He swallowed. 'Titus – the new emperor – he ruled Judea at that time. He gave the order to steal the temple treasure; to take all our sacred objects to Rome. The soldiers caught me, made me a slave, and brought me here, to Britannia.'

Taking a moment to look around at everyone, he said, 'Then yesterday, in the hospital, a soldier came in with a fever. He was raving. He said he'd killed a child from your tribe; a little girl. I went to the centurion, told him I'd heard a secret, and asked for Roman citizenship. Afterwards, he sneered, "Give you citizenship! A slave from Judea! I would die first." So – I had to escape.'

'Join us! Take revenge!' said Bryn. 'Rome is your enemy.'

Raphael shook his head. 'If I killed even one of them – I would be as cruel, as brutal as they are.' He sighed. 'Perhaps one day I can return to Judea. That's my dream.'

Turning to Mariad, he showed her some sprigs of lavender and rosemary.

'I've learnt about herbs and other medicines. I could help the tribe. May I stay – for a time?'

Aled looked over to the Seer. She nodded.

'Where's little Alys?' He glanced over at the children laughing and darting around the loaded carts.

A choking sound. Bryn put his head in his hands and walked away.

'Alys was his daughter,' said Aled. 'She was the child – the girl that was killed...'

Raphael froze. 'No! Oh no...'

The blacksmith took his arm. 'We're leaving for our hillfort by the sea. Come with us. The tribe welcomes you.'

Later, in the sacred grove, the Seer was chanting.

The time travellers waited. Tara was running her fingers over a moss-covered stone. Bethan dozed beside David as he flicked dead leaves with a twig. Simone was picking dandelions, blowing the seeds away, to be caught on the breeze.

Opening her eyes, the Seer spoke first to Simone. 'Girl from Rome. You did well. Two lives you saved.'

'*Si,* Yes. But—'

'And found the talisman.'

Next, she turned to David. 'Those poor suffering animals – you released them from misery.'

He stroked Bethan's ears. 'I made a bit of a mess...'

The Seer smiled. 'We come to this world to learn lessons.'

David coughed. 'Er – yes—'

The Seer studied Tara. 'Guardian of the Bronze Mirror. Dreamer, Peacemaker. Your second task is almost completed.'

Looking at the trio, she said, 'Your time here is ending. Continue with the quest – to save your world from destruction. Never give up. This planet is beautiful.' She reached under her cloak. 'But first—'

Twin! Do you think she's going to give us her golden torc?

David! You only ever think of treasure!

Smiling at him, the Seer touched the twisted golden coils around her neck.

Oh no! She's reading my mind...

'David. Take these most precious things.'

In her hand were some tiny brown objects with cups on the ends.

'Acorns!'

'Bury these acorns. Into mighty oaks they'll grow. Each will give breath to your world as it struggles to survive.'

'Thank you,' said David. He put them in his tunic pocket.

'And to fulfil your task here—'

Opening her leather pouch, she held up a long, pointed, pale purple crystal.

'The Amethyst Wand!' said Tara.

'Awesome!'

'Ammazza!'

'Keep it safe. It will protect you on your journey.'

Pausing, she gazed at them. 'Remain aware. Raging with anger is Mars, their god of war.'

Above the Seer appeared a rainbow, colours of every hue.

The Goddess!

'The portal opens. Go well.'

Along the track, up and down ditches, they made their way towards the burial mound. Bethan trotted next to David as he walked ahead with Edryn.

'We had some adventures.'

'Jumping into that freezing pool!'

'Spending a night in the dungeons!'

'I'll miss you, Edryn. I'll listen out for your poems...'

Mariad put her arm around Simone. 'We couldn't

have found the shield without you.'

'I'm sorry – I —'

'Together we succeeded.' She smiled at her friends. 'Now there's peace. That's what matters...' At the holly bush, she stopped. 'We can go no further.'

'I made up a song for you all – about the acorns,' said Edryn. 'Don't forget us – ever, will you? Look at the oaks, remember us...'

His voice rose in the air; soft and sweet.

'Summers and springs
Green leaves will they bring,

Seasons will pass
Yet the oaks will stand fast.
May they grow tall and strong
As the years are long,
Among grasses, and ferns.
We await your return...'

'Remember us...' Edryn's voice grew feint.

Mariad waved. 'Save your world... Go well!'

They began to fade; the veil shimmered.

'Go well!' whispered Tara. 'Goodbye, my friends...'

David strode ahead, his head down. Simone wiped tears from her cheeks and half turned back.

'They've gone, cuz.'

'I wish I hadn't been so—'

Tara hugged her.

Bethan stared up at her friends.

They look so sad. I'll run over to those trees.
They'll have to chase me. That'll be fun.

The puppy raced off towards the gorse bushes.

Twin! Bethan's disappeared.

I'll whistle. She'll come back in a second.

The portal is closing ...

Loud snorting came from the undergrowth as
Tara took the Bronze Mirror out of her bag.
Crashing sounds. A wild boar was charging; its
tusks aiming straight for her. Startled, she
stumbled, lost her grip on the Mirror and shouted,
'Don't let it drop! Catch it!'

Simone dived. As she caught the handle, she felt
herself falling.

A pair of fiery burning eyes bored into hers.
Mars! The Warrior God!

Down, down, into the portal she tumbled.

'Tara! David! Help!'

Simone felt the ground beneath her. Thistles.
Ouch!

She shifted; something hard and oval was lying
next to her.

The Bronze Mirror! I must give it to Tara now.
'Twins!'

The air smells different... kind of smoky...

A brown and white shape jumped on top of her and began nuzzling her neck. 'Bethan! Just one pat.'

As she stroked the puppy, she noticed her clothes. 'Jeans, T-shirt, my new sandals. The 21st century!'

She stared around. A clump of tall silver trees. Were they here before?

Where are the twins? Will the Mirror tell me? Am I allowed to ask?

But all she saw were grey-white mists swirling. No images. No whispers.

She trembled. *Have they been taken to another time – by Mars, God of War?*

High up in a silver birch, a blackbird was singing. Underneath, a squirrel was jumping from branch to branch.

'That was spectacular! A rollercoaster! said David. 'What century are we in, Twin?'

'Grey squirrel, white butterflies, vapour trails in the sky...'

'But the tell-tale sign is—'

'Your grubby old T-shirt and ripped jeans!'

The twins rolled around on the grass, laughing.

'We're back! It's the twenty-first century!'

Tara sat up. 'And what can I hear?'

'Barking!'

Bethan hurtled towards them and began jumping all over David.

'Hi, puppy. I missed you!' he said, scratching her head.

Simone ran over. 'I was so afraid that I'd never see you again.' Her eyes welled up. 'Where have you been?'

David grinned. 'We whizzed past Jupiter and Neptune, avoided a couple of asteroids, dodged several meteorite showers, got caught between two spirals of galaxies – they were about to collide – And then we were spinning towards a void, a supermassive black hole. Two, actually...'

Simone's eyes were huge.

'... being dragged towards this abyss. Sucked into—'

'Twin!'

'But then I remembered...'

David felt into his jeans pocket. 'Have I lost it?'

'Twin! You can't have—'

'Here it is!' He pulled out—

'The Amethyst Wand!' Simone gasped.

'I'd forgotten I had the crystal. It stopped us from tumbling into the void.'

'O Dio mio!'

'It was the scariest thing that's happened to me in aeons.' He grinned. 'Where are our sandwiches?'

'They'll be stale by now!' said Tara. 'Nearly two thousand years have passed!'

'Or a few hours! Search, Bethan! Food!'

The puppy sniffed, raced to a spot underneath a hedge and barked.

David went over and pulled out three backpacks.

'Good girl! Green. This is yours, Tara—'

Simone held the Mirror out to her cousin. 'Here – I—'

'Thanks for looking after it, cuz.'

'Hey! This sandwich is still pretty fresh. It must be the same day as when we left! Cool!'

They had eaten lunch and were lying back, staring up at the cloudless sky.

David threw up a piece of apple for the puppy to catch. 'So, the second task is completed.'

Tara looked into the Mirror.

Came the whisper:

Remember your vow;
Step inside the mound,
Listen for the sound...

'Someone is waiting for us...'

'Do we all have to go into the burial mound again?' asked Simone.

'Yes, we do, cuz. Come on.'

Brushing aside grasses and ferns, Tara went into the mound first. She held the Mirror in front of her. The same musty smell. Bones of all shapes and sizes were scattered all over the earthen floor. Mice scurried out of the way.

David followed with Bethan. Simone hesitated then took a few steps forward.

A whisper:

Wait for a while;
Wait for the child.

Minutes passed. Small fingers touched Tara's hands.

'My friends. I thank you.
No more sorrow, no more pain.
For too long here have I lain.
Justice for me, for my people, you found,
I am now free to leave this mound.
Free to dance towards the light,
I see it dazzling, so bright, so bright.
Dancing with joy, now I go –
To my ancestors… to home…'

David swallowed hard. 'That – that was a good thing we did, helping her—'

Came a whisper:

Now go deeper, into this mound;
Seek, for you will find on the ground…
Something…

'*Oh no!* The roof might fall on us again.'

'The wand's protecting us, cuz.'

Holding the Bronze Mirror tightly, Tara directed

its beams further down the passage. It was much narrower; the roof was lower.

'We're going to have to crawl,' said Tara. 'Keep close behind me.'

On hands and knees, they moved forward until it opened out into a larger chamber. Bethan darted ahead, sniffing at some curled bones lying on the earthen floor.

'Do you think that's a skeleton?' said David, disappointed.

'A what?' cried Simone.

Twin, will you keep schtum!

Simone stood up and brushed dried mud off her jeans. '*Argh!*'

'There must be something—' said Tara as the Bronze Mirror swivelled around the chamber. Its beams lit up the walls, the roof, and then – in the darkest place – it revealed something large; something—

'What is it?'

'Do you think–?'

'It could be—'

There, in the corner, on its side, was a large, round, black shape.

'Point the Mirror so we can see clearly, Twin.'

'It's the cauldron! From the fire.'

'*Oh!* I've pins. All over me – pins!'

'Tingles down your spine? Me too, cuz.'

'And mega goosebumps,' said David.

'Take the lid off, Twin.'

Bethan stuck her nose on it. *Doesn't smell of anything interesting...*

David knelt down and pulled at the lid. It was stuck. He tugged at it hard.

It flew off and he staggered back.

The trio stared in amazement at what had spilled out: necklaces, torcs, bracelets, earrings, brooches.

'And here's a model of an oak tree!' said Tara. 'Wow!'

'Totally cool!'

'Here for two thousand years,' whispered Simone.

'Our friends were the last people to touch them,' said David. He pointed to a golden torc.

'Eight twisted coils. The Seer gave this to us after all,' he murmured. 'Thank you...'

'David! Look at this!' Tara held up a bronze horse.

'Edryn's horse.' David bit his lip. 'Oh – what a friend he was.'

Simone picked up a bracelet. 'Mariad was wearing this on our last day.'

'Before they left for Llanmelin, they placed them in here.'

The trio looked at each other.

'So many gifts they've given us,' said Simone.

'This is immense,' said David. 'Shall we do a "finding treasure" dance?'

Tara laughed. 'It's a bit cramped in here, Twin!'

Simone took some jewellery from the bottom of the cauldron. Admiring the bear brooch, she said, 'It would look so good on my new yellow T-shirt.'

'Cuz! It's treasure,' said Tara. 'Put it all back in the cauldron. Leave it as we found it. We'll go to the museum now in Caerleon, and declare it.'

'Guys – do you realise?' David sat back on his heels. 'We've found a hoard! Like Sutton Hoo. This is – the Hartland Hoard!'

'Wait,' said Tara. 'We don't know who the owner of this land is. We haven't got permission to be here.'

'Yes. Could be tricky explaining we travelled back in time!' David fussed the puppy. 'It's like last time. Bethan found it – didn't you, girl? You couldn't ask anyone... You're our alibi!'

Tara. Could I keep the horse?

No!

Over the fields, over the river, swifts were whirling, drifting, gliding.

'I'm going to have culture shock.' Simone pushed her hair back as they crossed the bridge into Caerleon. 'I need to plait my hair. And my nails are very dirty.'

David rolled his eyes.

Tara coughed as the cars and lorries passed them. *Ergh! The smell... the noise...*

Walking towards a green mound, they noticed stone steps going down into an arena. People were wandering around, taking photographs.

'This is the amphitheatre!' said David. 'Imagine! I was here – fighting for my life!'

Bethan charged forwards, pulling him with her.

'Twin!' he called over his shoulder. 'Guess who's here!'

'Who?'

'All of them, actually.'

'David!'

'Our archey friends! Rhys and Isabelle are there, too. Come on,' David shouted. 'This is going to be fun!'

The archaeologists were digging and sifting the soil, while Tabitha was giving a talk to a study group.

'I – er – we're discovering many important artefacts here at Isca. Caerleon was a big port—'

Alan looked up from a trench. 'You lot again!'

David edged close to Tabitha.

'I believe,' she said, 'we'll find a large building just over there—'

'A temple,' said David.

'Go away!' she hissed. 'And take your pesky dog with you.'

A stocky man from the group stepped forward. 'What's that you're holding?'

Wheeling around, Tabitha glared. David was holding up the bronze horse.

'Isn't the enamelling brilliant?' he said. 'The Silures made it; the local Iron Age tribe. They lived all around this area before the Romans invaded.'

He launched into everything he knew about the fortress; the barracks, the number of pools in the Baths, the workshops...

'And the building over there – that was the Customs House.'

'How do you know all this, young man?'

He smiled. 'Oh, research.'

A spluttering noise came from the trench. Toby was stabbing at the soil with his trowel.

'Just got here. Telling everyone how much he knows.'

Stab. Stab.

'It's Toby, isn't it?' David grinned. *Ah, the stick-out ears.* 'If you move – just a metre – to your right, you should find some 1st century Roman coins. Buried when some soldiers—'

Twin! Schtum!

Toby threw down his trowel and stomped off.

Isabelle began feeling the soil with her fingers. 'Can you come over here for a minute, Rhys?'

'Are you a psychic archaeologist or something?' asked a woman from the group.

Don't you dare, Twin!

David grinned. 'My dog is.'

Tabitha's face was becoming redder and redder.

She switched on her off/on smile.

'Now, about the treasure I found last week at Trellech.'

David laughed. '*You* found? Bethan found!' He picked up the spaniel. 'This is the best archaeologist dog – ever! She discovered a golden casket from Limoges – it belonged to John of Gaunt. And inside was the most stunning crystal vase – 11th century. From Cairo, gifted to a European king – or queen – as a sign of peace.'

'Awesome!'

'It – they—' stuttered Tabitha.

'Have you taken it all to the portable antiquities, yet Tabs? You must do that within fourteen days. Isn't that the law?'

She glowered. 'I haven't had time yet.'

'Ah – Busy. We'll tell Ruth and Alan where the treasure is. Then we know it'll be in safe hands...'

Will you shut up, Twin!

'Treasure? You've found a hoard?' asked the stocky man.

'The Hartland Hoard, we're calling it. This bronze horse is just one of the many artefacts we found...'

'Cool!'

Simone joined her cousin. '*Ciao!* Hi. There's a golden torc, a brooch with a bear on it – I feel a Druid wore it on her cloak. And bracelets...'

'They're not Roman,' muttered Tabitha.

'The Silures were so creative,' murmured Ruth.

264

'And skilled,' added Alan.

'The style's called—'

'*La Tene*.' Alan called over. '*La Tene* design.'

'Wow!' shouted Isabelle. 'Here's a stash of Roman coins!'

'They're silver!' said Rhys. 'This is brilliant!' Brushing off the soil, he added, 'This one has a head of —'

'Augustus?'

Twin!

'Let me see,' said Tabitha, barging through the group.

Isabelle was examining another coin. 'This one's gold!'

Alan stared at it. 'Amazing! This could've come from the temple in Jerusalem. How strange.'

'Maybe a centurion took it, when the treasure was looted by the Romans. And he came here afterwards and dropped it,' said David.

Twin! Can you stop burbling!

'How did you guys find the hoard?' asked the stocky man. He narrowed his eyes. 'Where is it now?'

'Bethan, our very special puppy, was digging up there.' Simone waved vaguely towards the hillfort. 'Looking for bones, and she found so many beautiful—'

'Cuz!' Tara grasped her arm to lead her away. 'Don't say anything else!'

'You've disturbed the site.' Tabitha glared.

'Never do that. You must keep to the rules.'

Simone became Cleopatra. 'We haven't disturbed it. The hoard's still there. Safe. It's **you** that hasn't kept to the rules!'

Elita and Osian had arrived by the trench.

'What an extraordinary day you've had!' said Osian.

'So exciting!' said Elita.

Their grandchildren rushed over to see them. Bethan jumped up, wagging her tail furiously.

'Look at this bronze horse, Grandpa,' said David. 'It's very special.'

'We've brought you some news,' said Elita. 'Simone – your parents will be coming soon.'

Oh! That was my wish...

'And twins – news for you, too – when you get home,' said Osian. 'There'll be five new additions to the family...'

David was astonished. 'Five? Brothers? Sisters?'

'Rescue chickens!' laughed his grandfather.

'Cool! I'll name one Eggscalibur! Omelettes forever!'

The next day, they went for a walk along the river.

'That's great Alan and Ruth are looking after the

hoard,' said David. 'And they registered it with the museum.'

The spaniel was straining at the leash, trying to chase rabbits, squirrels – any creatures that moved.

'Behave, Bethan! We're going to puppy training lessons. You've forgotten all your training since you stayed at the hillfort!'

'It must've been all those deer bones she chewed on!' laughed Tara.

'Can you ask the Bronze Mirror what happened after we left the tribe?' said Simone.

'Sure. Let's sit down on this bench,' said Tara. 'There's no one around.'

As they peered into it, white mists whirled and parted.

'There's Mariad!' cried Simone.

This golden torc, a gift from the Seer.

For Tara, the warrior, who has no greed, knows no fear.

Edryn held up his horse.

To David – a gift – this horse I made.

May our friendship never fade.

David bent down and stroked Bethan's ears.

Mariad spoke again:

My bracelet to Simone, I give,

May you be happy as long as you live...

'*Oh!* My heart...'

As this image faded, another came: the Seer standing by open waters.

'That's the River Severn,' said David. 'She's at the estuary.'

'O Goddess! Receive this offering...'

Holding either side of the shield, Mariad and Edryn walked towards the waves.

They stood for a moment.

'For Boudica and the Iceni!' called the girl.

'For Caratacus and the Silures!' shouted the young bard.

Throwing it into the air, the shield spun once, twice, three times, before spiralling down onto the waves and drifting out to the open sea.

'Why did Mariad say that about the Iceni?' asked Simone.

'She was cousin to Boudica – warrior queen...'

Simone sighed deeply. *Perhaps I could be a warrior...*

'Now to complete our second task,' said Tara.

Came a whisper:

Where Afon Llwyd meets the Usk ,
Cast the wand before it's dusk.
Each must hold the amethyst wand,
Make a wish; create a bond.
For this planet to be saved.
This sacrifice must be made.

Rain clouds were gathering as they arrived at the tributary. Drops began to fall as each took turns to hold the crystal and make their wish.

First, Simone spoke. 'May we save the rainforests.'

'May we protect all animals,' said David. 'especially bears. No more cruelty.'

'May all the peoples in our world respect Nature,' said Tara.

She handed the amethyst crystal to her twin.

Up into the air, he cast the wand.

It shimmered; lilac, violet, purple, threads of red.

Then, merging into the rainbow reflecting on the waters, it vanished from sight.

The Goddess spoke. *Cleanse the rivers, the seas; purify the oceans.*

Along the riverbank, two people were walking a dog.

Bethan growled and started barking.

'That husky's a lot bigger than you!'

Voices drifted to them on the breeze.

'Did you hear about that stunning find on the Gwent Levels last week?'

'No.'

'Someone found a bark shield. Iron Age... Only one other of its kind in Britain...'

'Makes you wonder how it got there...

'And what other treasures are still waiting to be discovered...'

THE BRONZE MIRROR
is the first book in the series
SPIRALS OF TIME

Time travellers, Tara and David have been sent on a mission to save Planet Earth. Deep in the Wye Valley, they discover the mysterious Bronze Mirror. This sets them on an adventure to the wild Welsh Marches of the fourteenth century.

Along with their reluctant cousin Simone and puppy Bethan, they meet a family who desperately need help. A valuable document has been stolen and hidden in Monmouth Castle. Unless it's found the family will lose their home and their land.

With powerful forces, plots and dark secrets coming to light, the children race against time to crack a code and reveal a precious secret. Only then can they save the family's fortunes and begin their quest to save the planet.

In the face of increasing danger, will the Mirror return them to their own time before it's too late?

"Twins Tara and David and their cousin Simone are whizzed back to the fourteenth century in a fast-paced adventure set in the dramatic Monmouthshire countryside.

The sights, sounds – and smells – of the fourteenth century are colourfully imagined, complete with knights, a banquet, and an urgent puzzle to be solved. I was hooked."

Janine Amos, children's author

THE GOLDEN WEB
is the third book in the series
SPIRALS OF TIME

In this new story the twins, Simone and Bethan, continue their quest to save Planet Earth. Arriving at a civil war re-enactment, they are transported to 1646. It is the time of the civil war and Raglan Castle is under seige.

The time travellers are trapped here: they are in the greatest danger. Caught in a tangled web of lies and deceit they are faced with terrible decisions to make and secret codes to crack. What is so precious that they must save it? Surrounded by betrayal and strife, can they ever find a way back to the 21st century?

Coming soon...